DEAD VELVET CAKE

EMILY JAMES

STRONGHOLD BOOKS

This is a work of fiction. I made it up. You are not in my book. I probably don't even know you. If you're confused about the difference between real life and fiction, you might want to call a counselor rather than a lawyer because names, characters, places, and incidents in this book are a product of my twisted imagination. Real locales and public names are sometimes used for atmospheric purposes. Any resemblance to actual people, living or dead, or to businesses, companies, events, and institutions is completely coincidental.

Editor: Christopher Saylor at www.saylorediting.wordpress.com/services/

Cover Design: Mariah Sinclair at www.mariahsinclair.com

Published September 2020 by Stronghold Books

Ebook ISBN 978-1-988480-29-9; Print Book ISBN 978-1-988480-30-5

ALSO BY EMILY JAMES

Maple Syrup Mysteries

Cupcake Truck Mysteries

FREE TIPS FOR AMAZING CUPCAKES

Each book in the Cupcake Truck Mysteries includes a cupcake recipe, but even when you have a great recipe, baking the perfect cupcake can sometimes be hard.

To receive the top 10 tips for amazing cupcakes (inspired by the Cupcake Truck Mysteries sleuth, Isabel), sign up for my newsletter at www.subscribepage.com/cupcakes.

(If you're already a member of my newsletter, no need to worry. I've emailed you a link to the tips too!)

ule #1 of self-preservation: Never run toward a scream.

The raised woman's voice that cut through the thick afternoon air wasn't exactly a scream. It was more of a *don't touch me*, but it seemed like the ingrained human instinct would still apply. Your average person didn't run toward a cry for help. It's why the first thing women are taught for self-defense is to yell *fire* instead if you're being attacked. People will come if they think there's a wreak they can gawk at or if they might need to protect their property from a threat.

The voices reached me again. My stomach felt like it'd tumbled over a cliff, and I paused midway through locking down the flap on my food truck.

That instinct to run from danger kept people safe. Very few people will run toward danger to protect someone else. It's why I always believed that police officers and other first responders should be paid more than men whose only talent was to throw, catch, or whack a ball.

I finished securing the flap, every muscle in my back so tense they ached like I'd fallen on something unyielding.

The voice of Fear in my head told me I'd be stupid if I went toward the potential danger instead of away from it.

But that wasn't what I'd want someone to do if I were the one screaming. In fact, I'd be dead now if someone hadn't helped me when I needed it. Janie would be dead now too, and the world would be a much darker place without that little girl in it.

I quickly locked the door on my truck and pocketed my keys.

There was a very good chance I'd regret this, but I didn't want to be one of those people who heard a scream, did nothing, and read about a murder or rape the next day in the newspaper. How did those people justify it to themselves?

I marched toward where it seemed like the original call had come from. The closer I got to the corner, the louder the voices became. A man's and a woman's.

I slowed. Based on the volume of their voices, they were on the main street. No serious harm could come to someone out in the open like that. We were at the end of the lunch hour. The rush was down to a trickle, but the streets of the downtown business district were still far from empty.

I could head back without leaving the woman in any real danger surely.

"No," the woman's voice came again, clearer this time. "I don't *have* to do anything."

Her words sounded firm, but there was a tremor to her voice, as if she wasn't sure she could back up what she said.

Worse, I recognized the voice.

It belonged to Eve. She was one of my testers. If I had a new cupcake flavor available when she stopped by, she got it for free in exchange for honest feedback.

Even before she'd joined my small, brave team of testers, she'd once been kind to me when I needed it. I'd accidentally served her barbecue sauce on what should have been a cherries jubilee cupcake. Instead of being angry, she'd checked to see if I was okay.

I wouldn't have called us friends, but we chatted more than I did with almost any other regular who came to my truck.

She'd been at my truck not ten minutes ago and left with a strawberry shortcake cupcake.

I don't know if I'd have turned back had the voice belonged to a stranger, but I couldn't since it belonged to Eve. Turning my back on someone who'd once shown me a kindness wasn't something even Fear could convince me to do.

Silly as it probably made me look, I planted my hands on my hips and threw my shoulders back into a Superman pose for a second. According to an article in The Positivity Project, it was supposed to make you more confident. The article had been specifically talking about doing it in a bathroom stall before a job interview, but it should apply here as well.

I forged forward around the corner.

Eve stood on the sidewalk in front of me. A tall man with muscles visible even under his dress shirt held her by the wrist. His grip didn't look painfully tight, but the way she leaned back from him clearly said she wanted him to let go.

People slowed and swiveled their heads to watch the scene as they passed. No one had stopped.

My blood thrummed in my chest and buzzed in my ears. Interrupting wasn't my place. I wasn't big or strong. I certainly wasn't brave.

But if a normal person like me didn't say something when another person was in distress, what kind of world did that leave us? A world where men like my husband Jarrod won.

If this man was Eve's Jarrod, I wasn't going to let her suffer in silence the way I had. I certainly wasn't going to let him bully her back into submission.

I sucked in a breath big enough that my lungs seemed to stretch, and I practically stomped over to Eve's side.

The sunglasses that she always kept perched on the top of her head had fallen to the ground.

I scooped them up and held them out to her. "Are you okay?"

Eve's gaze flickered from the man to me. Her head shook a tiny bit. The movement was so small that had her earrings not swayed, I might have missed it.

"I'm fine," she said in contradiction to her head shake.

I leveled my gaze to the hold he still had on her wrist and back up. "Are you sure?"

The man dropped her wrist. "This is a private conversation."

My insides felt about as stable as melted chocolate. I really wasn't brave enough for this.

Apologize, Fear hissed in my head. *Walk away while you still can. This isn't any of your business.*

Despite Eve's words, the skin around her eyes was red and tight in a way that said she was trying not to cry.

I couldn't leave her here.

I just had to pretend I was Claire. No one messed with Claire. She was like an earthquake and a tsunami in a human body. That quality had terrified me when I'd first met her after being hired to cater her grandfather's hundredth birthday party, but the longer I'd known her, the more I'd come to respect it.

What would Claire say? Claire would tell him that if it was a private conversation, they should probably be having it in private.

As much as I might like Claire's bravado right now, I was no Claire.

My only other role model for tough situations was Nicole Fitzhenry-Dawes—a friend and criminal defense attorney who lived in a different town. Nicole would have had a brilliant diplomatic way out of this, tricking the man into believing that it was his idea to walk away.

Unfortunately, I wasn't Claire or Nicole. All I was good at was hiding and running.

And maybe being a bit deceptive in order to stay safe.

Fear might have had the right idea.

I plastered an I'm-no-threat smile on my face. "I'm sorry to interrupt." I shifted my gaze to catch Eve's for a second. "I think you forgot your wallet at my truck, Eve. I wanted to catch you before you got too far away. Could you come back and see if it's yours?"

My voice sounded only marginally steadier than Eve's. At least we had strength in numbers now.

She lowered a hand to her oversized purse. "My wallet?"

The confusion in her voice was so genuine that I wasn't sure if she believed me or if she was a better actress than I was.

"Mmm hmm," I said. "I think it's yours anyway." I tried to signal her with my eyes that this was her opportunity to get away if she needed it.

The look the man gave me said he thought some species of bugs were smarter than I was. "And you couldn't have brought it with you?"

At least he bought my ploy. I didn't know whether he was abusive to Eve or not, but he certainly thought he was the smartest person in any room, and that worked in our favor.

I dropped my gaze as if I should have thought of that. "I thought it'd be safer locked in my truck. I didn't want to risk losing someone else's wallet."

Come on, Eve, I silently urged. *We've talked enough times that you should realize I'm not this dense.*

The man huffed a sigh.

Something flashed across Eve's face. "That makes sense." Her voice pitched a little too high to be natural. "I'll run back with Isabel for a second."

The man's eyebrows drew down, making him look a bit like the hand-drawn pictures of Neanderthals in my old high school textbooks. It contrasted with the pressed shirt, trendy tie, and dress pants he wore. "Or you could be sensible and check your purse. If your wallet's in there, you won't waste any more time on this. If you were more careful with your belongings, we wouldn't even have to wonder."

Shoot. Checking in her purse made complete sense.

Eve opened her purse and poked around slowly with one finger. "I don't think it's in here."

The man snatched her purse from her hands. So much for the societal convention that men don't go into a woman's purse. Jarrod had never followed that rule either.

He pulled her wallet out immediately. "What's this then?" He shoved her wallet back in and tossed the purse at her. "What's going on here?"

I couldn't bring in enough air, as if I had a piece of cloth over my face. I stepped back before I could stop myself. Butting in to their argument had been foolish. If this guy turned out to be abusive, I'd now made this so much worse for Eve.

I should have known better.

The only thing you could do to help someone in an abusive situation was to get them out. Aggravating their abuser only made things worse.

Eve rolled her eyes. I think she meant it to lighten the mood, but she looked a bit like a spooked horse. "I don't have my contacts in. You know I can't see a thing without them."

She held out her hand to him, not meeting my gaze. I wanted to tell her how sorry I was. I wanted to tell her I should have known better. I wanted to tell her that if she wanted out permanently, I'd find a way to help her.

And I couldn't say any of it.

"We're already late." He took her hand, his grip tight. He turned a knife-sharp look on me. "Stay away from us, and mind your own business. People who butt in where they're not wanted make trouble for themselves."

I heard the threat underlying his words as clearly as if he'd stated it bluntly.

I couldn't meet up with him again, even accidentally. I couldn't risk that he'd follow through with his threat. I couldn't risk that Eve would stand up to him one day, and he'd blame me —seeking me out where he knew I'd be every day. I couldn't risk that he'd see us together even innocently and punish her for it later.

The best way to stay safe and to protect Eve was to give up my regular lunchtime spot and never return to it again.

2

*J*anie curled her feet up onto the dining room chair so that she looked a bit like a bird perched on a fence. The sit-squat was her usual routine for near the end of the meal, when she really wanted to move around, but knew she needed to wait.

Dan's cousin Claire—unlike usual—didn't reprimand Janie for it, and Dan simply pointed at her plate to remind her to eat as well as talk. I didn't say or do anything, even though her method of eating in a squat on a chair tended to make me worry she'd choke on something if she slipped. I'd been eating Sunday dinner with them for the past two months since we'd been thrown together by the murder of Claire and Dan's grandfather, but I wasn't really a relative. I didn't want to overstep my place.

Janie shoved a piece of roasted chicken into her mouth and gave a wiggle. "Which one do you think I should get Isabel?"

I shoveled a bite of now-cold green beans into my own mouth to buy myself some time. I hadn't been paying as much attention as I should have to Janie's chatter. Normally, hearing all about her week cheered me up even after the most lackluster day.

Today, my stomach felt full with the anxious feeling I'd had since my run-in with Eve and the man. My body didn't have room for anything else—thoughts or food.

But none of that was Janie's fault.

"Which one do you want more?" I asked.

Given enough time, she'd fill in the gaps over whether we were talking about stickers vs a bubble blower or whatever she'd been offered.

"I want both, but Daddy says I can only have either a puppy or a kitten, not both. I tried to tell him that six is old enough to take care of both. And you or Auntie Claire might still need to get me a birthday present so you could get me the one I don't get from Daddy."

Dan lifted his napkin to his mouth, but I caught a glimpse of a grin before he did. "You're only allowed one, at least until we see how well you take care of it."

Janie pouted out her bottom lip and swirled her remaining green beans around on her plate. I glanced at Claire, but she didn't even seem to notice.

"Okay." Janie's frown vanished as quickly as it'd come. She focused back on me again. "Which one would you pick?"

"I love both. Are you going to get them from the shelter where the ones who most need a home are?"

"Yup. Daddy says people forget about those ones, and they'll be the most excited to be in our family."

So the cost of the future pet wasn't an issue. The adoption fee from the shelter was minimal. What was probably more important here was which pet Janie would find easiest to care for long-term. Or which pet Dan would find easiest to care for if this experiment failed. I knew Dan was too responsible to abandon a pet simply because Janie didn't follow through on her promises.

I tapped my lips as if considering my answer. "You know doggies need to go outside to the bathroom even in the winter when it's cold."

She stared at me for a few seconds as if thinking that through. "And Daddy says I have to clean up the poopy of whatever I get."

"We don't talk about poopy at the table," Claire said, but it lacked its usual force.

This time I had to raise my napkin to hide a smile. It felt good to smile, like it was a release valve for life.

Janie hopped up so that she balanced on her toes. "Can I leave the table and go look at shelter kittens on the iPad?"

"Two more bites of beans," Dan said, "and remember that some of the kittens you see might already be adopted by the time we get there."

"Look at the older cats, too," I said. "They'll be the most excited to have a new home."

Janie shoved her mouth chipmunk-full with the rest of her beans and scuttled away before anyone could tell her to chew and swallow first.

Claire laid her silverware down on her plate even though she'd barely eaten anything. "You're going to regret that."

My normal policy was to avoid contradicting Claire. But tonight her comment felt like one more person trying to control another. Dan had clearly already made his decision about allowing Janie to have a pet. Claire didn't need to make him worry it'd been the wrong call.

"Pets are good for kids." I kept my voice soft so it at least wouldn't come across as an attack. "They learn responsibility and empathy."

Claire huffed, but didn't argue.

Dan shot me that smile of his that crinkled the corners of his eyes. Another knot of tension in my stomach floated away.

He shifted to face Claire. "That's the most you've said all night. What's going on?"

"You already know what." Claire swiped up Janie's empty plate and my nearly empty plate without asking if I was finished. She didn't move away once she had my plate in hand. "What about you? You've been abnormally quiet tonight too."

Dan hadn't seemed abnormally quiet to me, but Claire knew him better than I did.

Silence fell on the room, and I looked up. Both Claire and Dan were watching me. Oh. She wasn't asking Dan. She was asking me.

The part of me that'd been watching Claire and Dan dig into each other's lives in a method that would seem nosy if they weren't so close had wondered what it'd be like to have someone care about me that way again. Just a few months ago, I felt the hole in my life where people should have been—where I didn't even have someone to tell about my day.

The part of me that was used to having to hold everything inside said differently. It wanted to clamp down tighter than a lobster claw and claim everything was fine.

How could something I wanted so much still be so scary?

Claire glared at me with an expression that said *don't you dare lie to me*. I'd seen her use it on Janie before. My hesitation cracked. You didn't give that look to a stranger. She didn't think about me as a stranger anymore.

Or, at least, maybe I didn't have to keep being one. Maybe.

"I had to give up one of my regular spots." Sharing even that much felt as uncomfortable as streaking down the middle of the street. I wasn't about to tell her *why* I'd had to give it up. Baby steps. "My income's been down ever since. I'm...worried."

That was putting it mildly, but I couldn't bring myself to admit to feeling terrified. I'd been eating regularly again, and when my truck needed new brake pads last month, I'd been able to replace them. I didn't want to go back to eating one meal a day and praying my frayed tires would prove to be magically eternal.

Claire plopped the dishes into the sink. She turned back around and the expression on her face reminded me of my dad when I'd told him I'd tried my best, but I was still failing calculus. First he'd hugged me. Then he'd told me he'd failed calculus on his first try too. And then he'd sold our beater car, and we'd taken the bus for the rest of the year so he could hire me a tutor. Claire had that kind of look on her face now.

Something that felt a lot like hope filled my chest.

She planted her hands on her hips. "You should be doing the summer festivals. I can help out if you can't handle that volume by yourself. The sandcastle competition is next weekend, and then the hot air balloon festival is shortly after that."

The hope bubble popped as quickly as it'd formed. Yes, I'd be hard-pressed to serve people quickly in a high volume environment, but that's not what held me back from taking my truck to the big events Lakeshore held in the warm weather. "I applied when I first moved here. I'm on a wait list for next year for the sandcastle competition, but this year was filled six months ago. I'm still waiting to hear about the hot air balloon festival. The woman I spoke to didn't sound encouraging."

Claire scowled. If I hadn't known better, I would have thought she was as invested in fixing my problem as I was.

And maybe she was. Maybe by fixing my problem, she'd have

the hope or courage she needed for her own. The one that she didn't seem to want to talk about yet.

"That's not necessarily true," Dan said.

Claire and I turned to face him at the same time, as if he'd pulled strings attached to each of us. If I'd been on the outside looking in, it would have been funny.

"Which part?" I asked. "I was told that I couldn't just show up. There's limited spacing, and all the vendors need a special permit issued for the particular event."

"That's all true. But every year there are some last minute drop-outs. My station's running security for the sandcastle building, so I could put you in touch with the coordinator. There's only one catch."

Of course. Everything in life came with a catch. I raised my eyebrows, indicating he should go on.

"You'd need to be able to fill in on short notice, sometimes less than twenty-four hours."

I didn't care. If it meant bolstering my flagging income until I could find a new location for the lunch-time crowd, I'd do it.

3

*I*f I'd been asked to describe myself, over-ambitious wouldn't have been one of the terms I'd have chosen. But I felt like it suddenly should be after I ended the call with the coordinator of the twenty-fifth annual Lakeshore sand-castle-building competition.

Thanks to Dan connecting us, I had a spot.

What I didn't have was even twenty-four hours' notice. I had a bit over twelve. And seven to eight of those hours were ones I should have been using to sleep. I'd never pulled a baking all-nighter before, but I'd done the calculations and that's what I'd need to do to be ready for the competition tomorrow.

Calling Claire to see if her offer of help extended to a marathon baking session would have taken off some of the pressure. But Claire would inevitably wonder why we weren't baking the cupcakes in my apartment. Wouldn't we have had more counter space there?

Short of trying to make up some lie about my apartment being fumigated, I couldn't think up a believable reason. If Claire got suspicious enough, she'd push until she learned that I lived in my truck. I couldn't let that happen. Neither she nor Dan would want me to continue living in my vehicle, not to mention the health code violations. I'd be closed down if the wrong people found out.

No, I'd taken care of myself for this long. I could handle this event by myself. I'd go to my designated lot next to the beach where the sandcastle competition would take place, and I'd bake with the haste and fervor of a Food Network competitor.

THE SOUND OF A DIESEL ENGINE AND VOICES CALLING OUT instructions woke me. I jerked my head up from where it'd been resting on my countertop. My neck ached, my cheek felt sticky, and my eyes burned like I'd rubbed dirt into them.

I couldn't have been asleep long. I'd finished up the last batch of buttercream, and I'd sat down for just a minute to rest before I started decorating. Normally, I didn't like to prepare too many cupcakes in advance. Today, with the crowds the sandcastle competition website said they drew every year, I was expecting to have to serve at a rapid pace without many breaks.

I stretched and opened my door. The sound I'd heard was the organizers arriving. They had a temporary tent partway erected, and a table set up where competitors would get their numbers and lot assignment.

When Claire and Dan had first mentioned a sandcastle competition, I'd thought it would be mostly children or families. This was more like the American Ninja Warrior of sandcastle building. The competitors didn't just build castles. They built dolphins, octopii, a Medusa head surrounded by snakes, and castles that looked like recreations of the real thing, right down to windows and stones. Last year's winners had constructed a dragon that looked like it could have come to life.

It was hard to believe that the pristine, roped-off sections of beach in front of me would be able to transform into works of art in such a short amount of time. Working this event was probably going to be the most fun I'd had in years.

A taco food truck rumbled in to park five spaces down from me.

I popped open the front flap of my truck so I could watch everything come to life and set to work on decorating. It was too bad my Russian piping tips hadn't arrived in time. With the short notice, I didn't have time to pipe any buttercream flowers for decorations, and the Russian piping tips claimed to be able to create multi-colored flowers over the top of a cupcake in mere minutes.

While I filled and piped and turned the leftover bits into cake pops to set in the fridge for later in the afternoon, the spaces along the beachfront grew crowded, reminding me a bit of a farmer's market or county fair.

The slots between my truck and the taco vendor filled up with a woman selling beaded jewelry, and a husband and wife selling essential oils and all the gadgets that go along with aromatherapy. The mayor had a booth with calendars and individually wrapped chocolates—an amateur move in this kind of heat—reminding people to vote for him in the upcoming election.

The smell of freshly popping kettle corn wafted on the air along with the moist seashell scent I always associated with the water.

The early morning sun glittered off the ripples and caught me in the eyes. I squinted. If this went well, maybe I could afford to buy myself a new pair of sunglasses. The arm had popped off of mine, which probably shouldn't have surprised me since I bought them at the dollar store. This time, I'd like to get a pair that wouldn't rub the sides of my nose raw if I wore them for more than a couple hours.

The sun shifted, and my vision cleared. A petite woman with dark hair and sunglasses perched on top of her head bobbed past. She had a Rigman & Associates Insurance sign under one arm, flapping slightly in the breeze.

Eve?

I couldn't get a clear look at her face. That'd be just my luck.

The last thing I needed was for Eve to be here, manning her company's booth, and for her boyfriend or whoever he was to show up.

Hopefully, if he did, he'd be rational enough to realize that I wasn't here to cause him trouble. I was here working, like everyone else.

My throat felt tight. What would I do if he caused a scene and I lost customers...or even my place here.

I forced my focus back onto piping the strawberry buttercream onto my strawberry shortcake cupcakes. I couldn't think about that now. It might not even happen. It might not have even been Eve.

And with the competitors filing out into their designated parts of the beach, it wouldn't be long before the crowds grew. Cupcakes might not seem like a morning food, but I knew from my time working near the beaches in Fair Haven, that if you put fruit in it, people would start buying at around mid-morning.

The group of two men and one woman who took the allotment of sand almost directly in from of my truck had big number three armbands wrapped around their biceps and matching t-shirts.

One of the man wheeled a wheelbarrow full of supplies, and the other two competitors carried shovels and rakes.

As much as I wanted a long line of customers, I almost hoped there might be small breaks as well. And not only so I could do any small prep tasks. I couldn't imagine how the images I'd seen online could be built and sculpted from sand. It seemed like magic. I wanted a bit of a chance to watch it happen.

The burliest of the men on Team 3 picked up one of the shovels and spaded it into the sand. It stopped partway in.

He frowned and waved at the other over. "Just our luck. We got driftwood or something down a foot or so."

"Too many pieces of that and we'll have to complain," the woman said.

I suppose that made sense. My only experience with competition was what I used to watch on TV cooking channel shows. Those often cared more about good TV than fairness. In real life, it seemed like everyone should be given a block of sand to build that was equally easy to work with.

The woman and the other man grabbed their shovels and dug in.

The second man poked his shovel in, moved down, and poked it in again. "This might be too big for us to move. We might need a different spot."

Shoot. If that happened, I'd lose my front row seat.

A couple came up and ordered two cupcakes, taking my attention away. The woman joked that anything with fruit in it should count as breakfast.

"Of course," I said brightly. "If you want me to give you a reason why another variety should count as lunch, just come on back."

She smiled so big at the man next to her that her eyes crunched up.

"Nope," he said. "You promised if we got cupcakes for breakfast we could get pickles on a stick for lunch."

A scream broke the air before the woman could reply.

And it didn't stop.

What was going on? Whoever was screaming sounded terrified, like Jaws had jumped up out of the lake.

I craned my neck.

The woman from Team 3 had stepped back from where she'd been digging. Her shovel lay on the ground. Her hands covering her mouth barely muffled the keening still coming from her throat.

The organizers were running toward the site from one direction, and the officers who'd been walking the opposite way a moment before had turned back and were sprinting that way too.

One of the organizers skidded to a stop next to the woman and cursed.

He spun back around to the approaching police officers. "It's a body."

The man and woman who'd been in front of my truck moved toward the gathering crowd. I'd thought Eve seeing me would be the worst thing that could happen today. I'd been wrong.

The police were shouting at the crowd to stay back, and one

of the officers was on his cell phone, presumably calling in the situation.

I started packing up the cupcakes I'd set out. The competition wasn't continuing today, and I wasn't sticking around to see how this turned out. I couldn't afford for everything I'd baked to have to be sold tomorrow as day olds. And the last thing I wanted was to be questioned about yet another dead body.

At this rate, I'd have to change my sign from advertising *red* velvet cake to offering *dead* velvet cake.

4

The man in the suit had been sitting on the park bench near my truck for the past ten minutes as I worked my way through the line of customers. Even though he wore sunglasses and I couldn't see his eyes, I got the feeling that he was watching me.

Maybe it was simple paranoia. I almost always felt like someone was watching me. And most people wore sunglasses this time of year.

The suit man might just be uncomfortable with such a large crowd of children. A crowd of children who easily outnumbered the women with them were taking their time picking which cupcakes they wanted. They were all barefoot, having just come up from swimming, damp, sandy towels draped around their shoulders.

For me, seeing so much joy next to a beach would—I hoped—

eventually help me forget that someone had used a similar beach to bury a dead body. That hope was a large part of why I'd decided to try a beach-side location as a potential new spot to replace the one I'd lost. I didn't need another bad memory to follow me around. I didn't want to live my life haunted by ghosts that weren't even mine.

The crowd of women and children paid and wandered off toward the grass at the edge of the sand, where the women tried to convince the boys and girls to lay out their towels and sit before eating. Only partially successfully.

The suit man rose languidly from the bench, stretched, and ambled over to my truck as if it were the most natural thing in the world for someone to wait until everyone left rather than stand in line.

The moisture that had built at the base of my hair from the heat suddenly felt cold.

A few months ago, when I'd helped Dan figure out who killed his grandfather, my real name had ended up in the police files. Jarrod had called Dan's precinct. Even though Dan had thrown him off my trail for now, that didn't mean Jarrod couldn't have hired a private investigator to poke around in Lakeshore just in case.

The man stopped in front of the truck's order window. He pushed his sunglasses up off his face and pulled aside his jacket. Beneath hung a gun holster.

And a police detective's badge.

Relief with a pinch of uncertainty flooded through me. He probably hadn't been sent by Jarrod. He had to be here about the dead man at the sandcastle competition. I couldn't think of any other reason why a police officer would show up at my truck. I also couldn't think of what I could possibly add to the investigation into how a body ended up buried at a public beach.

"I'm Detective Strobel, Ms. Addington. Would you be able to join me out here for a few minutes?" He inclined his head toward the bench where he'd been sitting in the shade before. "You'll still be able to watch for customers, and I have a couple quick questions for you about the body that turned up at the sandcastle competition this past weekend."

I nodded and climbed out of my truck mechanically.

I didn't need to panic. I hadn't had anything to do with the body other than that I'd seen the competitors dig it up. And this detective called me Ms. Addington, so my real name wasn't going to end up in another police report where Jarrod would be able to find out that I was still in Lakeshore.

I did *not* need to panic.

He sank down onto the bench and patted the spot next to him as if there was somewhere else for me to sit, and I might not realize I should sit next to him.

"I talked to the organizers of the competition, and they told me your truck was parked directly across from the plot where the body was found. Is that correct?"

My mouth suddenly felt tight, like I'd sucked directly on a

lemon. Why did this feel more like he was leading me into a trap than merely interviewing me as a witness?

But there wasn't anything I could say other than the truth. "That's right. I was serving customers when the body was found, but I saw them start digging."

Detective Strobel nodded his head. "What time did you arrive that morning?"

"I was there the whole night, baking in preparation." I could hear the hesitancy in my own voice. I knew I should control my tone, but his approach made me think the truth was somehow going to stab me in the back. "I was given a spot last minute, and I didn't have enough cupcakes ready for the expected crowds."

He nodded as if everything I said matched with what he already knew.

My body wanted to relax, but Fear screamed that he was lulling me into a false sense of security. I tried to turn my back on the voice. I'd decided not to let Fear control me anymore. Besides, what could I do? I had been there baking all night.

"Did you see or hear anything? Anything at all while you were there?"

That sounded like he thought I should have.

I shook my head. "It was deserted until the organizers showed up about an hour before the competition was supposed to start."

"And you were there the whole time?"

I'd just said as much. The muscles in my arms tensed. Jarrod used to like to describe the techniques he used when interrogating a suspect or a criminal. Repeating the same question in different ways to see if he could trip them up was one of them.

"I was there the whole time."

He hmm'ed. "So that presents me with a problem, Ms. Addington. Time of death shows that you would have been there at the time when the victim died, and our medical examiner says that it's unlikely the body was moved postmortem. The murder happened on site or very close by."

The air suddenly felt too thick to fit down my throat. He was saying that the murder happened right in front of me. Or, at the very least, that the body would have had to be buried there while I was baking in my truck.

I should have heard something. Despite the heat of the oven, I'd had my flap down to keep out mosquitos. That wouldn't have blocked out the sound of a murder, though. I hadn't been playing music. Why hadn't I heard anything?

Oh. No.

The police were asking the same thing I was. I didn't have an answer for them. But I knew the answer they suspected. They thought I had either witnessed something and was too afraid to speak or that I was somehow involved in the murder.

"I fell asleep for about fifteen or twenty minutes right before the organizers arrived. The noise they made woke me up." Even after all my years with Jarrod, I didn't know how best to modulate my voice with this much blood pumping through my veins.

Too calm and they wouldn't believe me. Too shaky and they wouldn't believe me. My voice came out somewhere in the middle, reedy and thin.

Detective Strobel hmm'd again deep in his throat. I could almost see the disbelief floating around him in a cloud. If the organizers had woken me up, surely a murder and someone digging a man-sized hole would have. Assuming that fifteen or twenty minutes was even enough to kill someone, dig their grave, and bury them back up.

"Do you know anyone by the name of Anthony Rigman?" he asked, his voice mild, as if this were a formality.

I hadn't expected the body to belong to someone I knew—I knew very few people in Lakeshore—but it was still a relief. I felt like I'd heard the name Rigman before, though. If I couldn't place it, I couldn't have heard it in more than a passing context. I certainly didn't have a personal connection.

"No," I said, my voice calm for the first time since he showed up, "I don't know an Anthony Rigman."

He tilted his head to one side as if examining a strange piece of modern art and trying to figure out what it was supposed to represent. "Are you sure? Because I have witnesses who said they saw you arguing with him a couple weeks ago."

Arguing with him?

I gave myself a mental shake. Repeating back to myself the things Detective Strobel asked wasn't helpful. But I hadn't had an argument with anyone other than Eve's male companion.

My hands went cold like I'd stuck them in a bucket of ice. Eve had been carrying a sign that said Rigman & Associates at the sandcastle competition. "Do you have a picture of the victim?"

I didn't even bother trying to control my voice this time. If my suspicions were right and Anthony Rigman was Eve's boyfriend, I'd be in real trouble. Many people saw me shove myself into their argument.

On top of that, I'd practically run from the scene once the body was found. Leaving quickly had been a practical choice. I'd had a fridge full of cupcakes, more than I could normally sell in three days. To recover any of my costs, I'd needed to move quickly to try to sell them.

To the police, fleeing when a body is found looks an awful lot like guilt.

Detective Strobel patted his suit pocket and came up with a photo. He handed it over to me.

I glanced at it and flinched. Not only had the image clearly been taken of the dead body while it lay in the morgue, but it was also the man Eve had been arguing with.

I was screwed.

I handed the photo back to Detective Strobel. "I didn't know his name, but I recognize his face. I only met him once. He was with one of my regular customers."

Detective Strobel tucked the picture away. "And what was the argument about?"

"It wasn't so much an argument as..." As what? As what, Isabel? I wanted to shake myself for being so stupid. By downplaying the interaction, I sounded even more guilty. "I heard a man and a woman arguing, and I was concerned for the woman's safety. So I intervened."

"You were concerned for the safety of a woman out in daylight on a public street?" The skepticism in his voice was so thick it was amazing he could get the words out.

A tiny spark flared up inside me. Women were accosted on public transit in daylight all the time. They were harassed in their offices. They were abducted from grocery store parking lots in broad daylight.

And attitudes like Strobel's were part of what stood in the way of making our world one where a woman could feel as safe as a man.

I lifted my chin slightly. "Yes. I was worried about her. I went to make sure she was okay, and Mr. Rigman wasn't happy that I interfered in their conversation."

"I thought you said you didn't know his name."

My breath stumbled over my words so that neither worked properly. He thought I was lying about how I'd met Anthony Rigman. Nothing I could say today was probably going to change that. But if I wasn't careful, he could ask me to come down to the police station and give my fingerprints and a DNA sample.

Whatever else happened, I couldn't allow that to take place. Not only would the revelation that Isabel Addington wasn't my real name make me look more guilty, but putting myself into the system would put a flashing GPS signal on me for Jarrod to find me. The last case I'd been accidentally involved in, where my fingerprints ended up in the system, proved that. I'd only been able to avoid Jarrod that time because Dan lied to him and told him that he thought Amy Miller had left town.

I swallowed down the bubble of panic that tried to shoot up my throat. "I didn't know his name at the time. You gave it to me now."

Detective Strobel mmm'd again, and I had the desire to ask him if he needed a throat lozenge. "And what were they arguing about?"

If the police were looking at me, they were likely looking at Eve too. Telling the police that I didn't actually know what their argument was about was going to make me sound more guilty, as if I were covering for her or as if we'd killed him together.

Unfortunately, there wasn't anything else I could say but the truth. I certainly wasn't going to sacrifice her by making something up only to save myself. Besides, if she had killed him, any lie I might make up could mislead the police and prevent an arrest.

All I'd wanted to do was protect someone who might have been in trouble. No good deed, it seemed, went unpunished.

"I couldn't hear the whole argument. I mostly heard raised voices. All I know is that she wanted him to stop or to let her go."

"I see." Detective Strobel dropped his sunglasses down over his eyes. "I'll have more questions for you in the future, Ms. Addington. You're a surprisingly hard woman to find considering you run a business. I'd appreciate it if you gave me your phone number and home address."

I nodded so slowly it probably looked like my neck was stiff. I couldn't give him a home address.

I listed my phone number off one number at a time, making sure he'd written it down before giving him the next one. Then I had him read it back to me.

"And your address," he said.

I was out of time to think of something. Chances were good that he wouldn't show up at whatever address I gave him. Even if he did, I could always pretend he got it wrong. Or, at least, I could if I gave him an address next to one where I could pretend to live if it came to that.

I rattled off the neighbor next door to Claire's house.

Hopefully he wouldn't ever check. The last thing I wanted was Claire and Dan finding out that I lived in my truck.

"Have a nice day, Ms. Addington." He doffed an imaginary hat and strolled away.

Something about the way he did it made me think of Humphrey Bogart and that signature hat he wore. My dad loved the black-and-white Humphrey Bogart movies like *Casablanca*. He'd always said modern movies depended too much on special effects at the expense of characters.

I blinked back the press of tears. Memories of my dad always seemed to hit me at the least suitable times. Though, perhaps, it was that I thought of him whenever I needed advice.

Fear was shouting at me to run again.

I climbed back into my truck and leaned against the counter where I had a good view of the women collecting up the gaggle of children. They were all around Janie's age. Janie whose whole-hearted joy, enthusiasm, and love gave me something to look forward to.

I'd lost so much. I didn't want to lose Janie. Or Dan. Or even Claire, despite the fact that I couldn't tell if she liked me or not.

I didn't want to start over again. Dan and Claire knew my name wasn't really Isabel Addington, and they were willing to protect me by keeping my secret.

So I wouldn't leave this time.

I whispered the words out loud to myself to help them stick. I was staying.

At least, I was staying for now. If it got to the point where the police were going to arrest me for a murder I didn't commit, I might not have any choice other than to run.

5

"I'll buy the rest of what you've made for today if you'll close up and talk to me."

I jerked upright from the position I'd been in with my head stuck into my truck's small fridge and smashed the crown of my skull on the shelf above. I yelp and pressed a hand to the radiating pain.

"Are you okay?" the same woman's voice asked. "I didn't mean to scare you."

I turned around, my vision still a bit spotty at the edges. Eve peered at me over the counter of my food truck.

With her boyfriend dead, I'd gone back to my usual lunch spot. He wouldn't care now. But I felt a little guilty benefitting from his death. Still, what good would staying away have done. It'd have been a bad business move, especially considering that I hadn't been able to sell all the cupcakes I'd made for the sandcastle competition. Not even close. Not even as day-olds. I'd ended up taking a bunch to Dan and Janie and then another batch over to Claire. Dan had tried to pay me, and I'd been so desperate that I let him.

"May I come inside?" Eve glanced back over her shoulder. "Before any other customers show up. Or we could take a walk."

Her speech was coming too quickly for my bumped brain to sort through. "I have dozens of cupcakes left."

"That's okay." Eve pulled out a wad of cash that would more than cover what my remaining cupcakes would cost. "I don't mind, and this can't wait. I've been watching for you every day."

Coming from almost anyone else, that might have sounded ominous. Coming from Eve, I couldn't hear it that way. Her sunglasses were back on top of her head, holding back her hair, and her petite height meant she could barely see over the counter.

With her sunglasses up, I could clearly see her eyes. They looked tight the way people tended to tense the muscles at the corners of their eyes when they were focusing hard on something. Or when every muscle in their body was also tense.

Her eyes weren't red-rimmed or puffy. She didn't look like she'd been crying at all despite Anthony Rigman's death.

If I noticed it, the police would have too. That didn't bode well for her.

But aside from all that, I saw the woman who could have

written me off when I put barbecue sauce on her cherries jubilee cupcake and hadn't.

I pushed the money back toward her even though I could have used it. "I'll lock up."

I shut everything down and stepped out to join her on the sidewalk. I dropped the flap into place and locked it as well.

Eve led the way down the side street, away from the main road and toward a small park. Lakeshore was full of them. This one had a few benches under trees and a memorial to the men from Lakeshore who'd fought and died in the World Wars.

Eve fiddled with her sunglasses, sliding them up and down on her face as if she couldn't decide whether to wear them or use them to keep her hair from blowing into her face. "So, the thing is, I was hoping you wouldn't say anything about that argument you interrupted a couple weeks ago, between Anthony and me. If anyone asks."

Strike two for Eve's innocence. Not that it was any of my business. I wasn't the police or a jury. I had no right to judge what had or hadn't happened.

"The police already talked to me." I felt like a traitor even though I hadn't done anything wrong. "They had other witnesses who saw the argument too."

Eve gave a quick bob of her head. "I wondered if they would. A lot of my co-workers walked by while it was happening."

My brain rolled that over and couldn't think of anything to say. Eve seemed like a nice person. She'd been kind to me anyway. Yet her co-workers walked by. They didn't stop to help her or make sure she was okay.

That couldn't be typical. To have no allies at all among your co-workers.

Normally, I wouldn't have pried, but I was a suspect. If Eve was guilty, I'd like to know. Even if she wouldn't say as much directly, if I could settle it in my own mind, I'd know whether I needed to avoid her or not. With the police already looking at me, being seen with the real murderer wouldn't exactly clear my name—or my pseudonym as the case might be.

"Why didn't any of your co-workers stop?" I flinched. As soon as the words were out, I could hear how rude it sounded. Rude and suspicious.

Eve looked like a little girl whose friends avoided eye contact while a bully teased her on the playground. "Anthony's... Anthony was our boss."

So they'd chosen to protect themselves rather than protect Eve. My analogy about the bully on the playground wasn't that far off. Evil people stayed in power through that fear and desire to protect ourselves above someone else.

Eve took off her sunglasses and shifted them from hand to hand. "The police think I killed him because I wasn't suspicious when he didn't call me from the conference he was supposed to be at. I thought he was still angry from the argument you inter-rupted, and I was enjoying my time to myself. What girlfriend wouldn't miss her boyfriend, the police asked me? I didn't have an answer."

Her words flooded out fast but not defensive. More like she desperately wanted to tell them to someone who might actually believe her.

Like she thought I would believe her because I'd stepped in to stop Anthony that day on the street.

I wasn't a hero. I certainly wasn't brave. I lived with my fear every single day while I hid from my abuser.

And I knew that living with that over a long period of time could push a person to do things they otherwise wouldn't have done. I'd sometimes daydreamed about getting to Jarrod's gun quick enough when he hit me to shoot him. Maybe that made me a bad person. It certainly meant I wouldn't judge Eve if she'd killed Anthony. I wouldn't help her lie to the police or dodge prosecution, but I wouldn't judge her. Whether it was right or wrong, I wouldn't tell the police what she told me either. If they wanted to charge a woman for murdering an abusive partner, they'd have to figure it out on their own.

Since she seemed to think I was the closest thing she'd get to an ally, she might tell me everything if I approached slowly so as not to spook her. At least then I'd know how worried I needed to be about the police investigating me. "Did he hit you?"

Eve's mouth dropped open in a way that would have been comical under any other circumstances. "No!" Her gaze slipped to the side, and she rolled her lips together. "He liked to tell me that I would deserve it if he did, though. He said if he wasn't such a good man, he'd have beaten some sense into me." Her voice was soft and vulnerable. "But I didn't kill him. I can't even empty my own mouse traps."

If I were wrong, God would need to forgive my foolishness because I believed her. I probably shouldn't have. I knew better than almost anyone that people weren't always what they appeared to be.

Eve just sounded like she'd believed him when he told her those things. She didn't sound like someone who'd reached the end of their ability to cope with the abuse. She hadn't taken the out I provided that day I interrupted their argument.

She'd been under his control up until she'd found out he died.

"Do you believe me?" she asked, her voice still small.

She was in so much trouble. Her meekness and kindness seemed to run so deep that there was no way the police would believe it was genuine.

But I did. I nodded. "I think the police suspect me too. His body turned up on the beach, right in front of my truck, at the start of the sandcastle competition."

Eve flinched like she'd been stung by a hornet. "I was there. The insurance firm where I work had a booth."

I'd been right that I spotted her that day.

"I didn't find out that the body those competitors dug up was Anthony until my other boss called me." Eve stuck the end of her sunglasses into her mouth, hesitated like she hadn't realized what she was doing, and pulled them out again. "I don't think the police are considering anyone else for the murder."

The police had two solid suspects between Eve and me. She was the verbally-abused girlfriend who had what would sound like a shaky reason for why she hadn't worried when he didn't call. I was the woman who confronted him publicly and was threatened by him, then conveniently was at the scene of his murder without hearing or seeing anything.

Given my rescue of Eve, the police probably did think we were in on the murder together. I didn't know how the legal system worked when the police suspected a conspiracy.

It seemed like finding evidence to prove one of us guilty would help prove the other one guilty. If we were both arrested and neither of us confessed, we'd also be tried together.

In other words, Eve and I were suddenly linked in a way that we couldn't extricate ourselves from.

We turned around and walked back toward my truck in silence.

"I don't know what to do," Eve finally said. "I didn't kill him, and I don't believe you killed him. You didn't have any reason to. But if we're the only two they're investigating..."

If we were the only two the police were investigating, then our odds weren't good. One or both of us could be charged with a crime we didn't commit.

I'd been here before, accused of something I hadn't done and feeling like I had to stick up for myself because no one else would.

Despite my relationships with Dan and Claire, this wasn't their fight. They might support me morally, but they didn't have the ability to protect me from suspicion. Not even Dan, who likely worked with or knew of the detective in charge of the investigation. I couldn't expect him to risk his professional situation for my sake. I was basically a stray he'd taken in out of pity.

I'd discovered in the past, though, that I could sometimes have more success figuring out who'd committed a crime than the police could. People suspected me less because I wasn't wearing a badge. I could investigate more deeply because I didn't have multiple crimes to look into. And I wasn't held back by protocol and traditional investigative techniques. I could act as a maverick.

If Eve and I could find some reasonable alternative suspects, I was sure Dan would at least be willing to present those as options to the police.

I stopped, and Eve copied me, turning back around to face me. Hopefully her adventurousness extended further than trying new cupcake flavors.

"I have an idea, but it's unconventional."

6

"*I* don't have a key to Anthony's house," Eve said after I'd explained my idea that we should come up with a list of viable alternative suspects for the police. "He didn't want me being able to go in on my own even though I stayed over a few times a week. It always made me suspicious. Maybe we should start there and see if he was hiding anything at the house."

If he had been, the police had likely found it and logged it into evidence by now. That said, they could have overlooked something important because it didn't look relevant. Eve might notice something they hadn't.

Besides, I didn't have a better idea for where to start.

Anthony wanting Eve at his place when he chose and not any other time smacked of control again if nothing else.

I hadn't studied psychology or counseling. I didn't know

about abuse in general or whether all abused partners stayed for the same reasons. This was the first time I'd spoken to someone who'd been in even a remotely similar situation.

But Eve seemed so different from me. She had a good job. She appeared confident and fashionable. She wasn't the kind of woman you'd guess would end up in an abusive relationship.

I'd always thought that there was something wrong with me that I'd ended up trapped the way I did. If it could happen to someone like Eve, maybe what I'd experienced with Jarrod hadn't been because I'd been too weak or too stupid or too incompetent.

Maybe what happened was something that could happen to anyone given the right set of circumstances.

"My husband wasn't a good man, and it took me a long time to get up the courage to leave," I said so she'd know that my question wasn't an accusation. "Why did you stay?"

"I didn't feel like I had any other option." Eve shrugged and pressed the clicker to unlock her car. "He was my boss. He'd fired people for a lot less than breaking up with him, and I didn't want to lose my job. At Rigman & Associates I'm the head of the marketing department. It's incredible creative freedom." She laughed in a way that sounded self-conscious. "That makes me sound like I'm sleeping my way up the ladder, but it wasn't like that. It was after I was hired. And he was kind at first. Sometimes he was still kind."

Her last words were soft and sad. It was the first hint of

sadness at Anthony's death that I'd seen from her. I understood that too. Even when she hated him for how he treated her, she still also loved him on some level—a level that would never make sense to anyone who hadn't lived it.

The echoes between her story and mine made me feel like someone had pinched my heart. "I think that's part of how they get you to stay. You convince yourself that those glimpses of kindness are who he really is."

Eve blinked rapidly and nodded her head.

The longer I talked to her, the more I wanted to make sure neither of us were blamed for something we didn't do. Anthony had likely been killed for something he'd done. Eve shouldn't have her freedom taken away from her due to his choices.

We needed a way into Anthony's house to look around that didn't involve breaking-and-entering. "Do you know any of his family members who might have had a key to his house? We could tell them you left some of your stuff there and need to pick it up."

Eve straightened, reminding me of a wilted flower that'd been given a drink of water. "I know the name of the woman who cleans his house. She has a key."

ANTHONY'S CLEANING LADY TURNED OUT TO BE A PALE WOMAN IN her fifties who was so skinny and pointy that I wasn't sure how she'd manage to carry a vacuum from one floor to the next. She had a handkerchief tied around her head, a few wisps of blonde hair sticking out the front.

Eve had barely closed the door to her car when the woman threw her arms around her. She pinned Eve's arms to her sides.

"Oh, Evie, I'm so sorry. He was such a good man. I don't know who would do something like this."

Eve micro-flinched, the way I used to when someone would tell me what a good man Jarrod was and how lucky I was to be married to him. The movement was small enough to go unnoticed by most people, almost like a muscle twitch.

The woman let Eve go and looked over at where I stood near the hood of the car. I took a step back. No offense to a woman who seemed nice enough, but I didn't let strangers hug me.

She linked her arm with Eve's. "I'm glad you brought a friend for moral support. That'll make it go quicker. I still have another house to get to tonight, so I don't have long."

Her final house must be one she cleaned while a family was out of the way for a regular weeknight activity. We'd scheduled our chance to get into Anthony's house late in the day when Eve would be done work and I wouldn't miss out on much for customers.

Our plan was for Eve to distract Anthony's cleaning woman in one part of the house while I snooped in another under the guise of checking for anything Eve might have left lying around in a random room. Ideally we'd have been able to get into the house and look around without anyone watching us. According to what Eve told me after she called the cleaning woman, that was off the table. The woman seemed to think she was doing Eve a favor by staying the whole time, and Eve wasn't able to convince her she didn't need to.

The woman's insistence actually made sense. Eve shouldn't need a lot of time to gather her belongings from a home she only visited and didn't live in. I wasn't sure how these situations normally went, but she couldn't have more than a dresser drawer of clothes and a few items in the bathroom.

I'd have ten or fifteen minutes at best.

"Most of my things should be upstairs," Eve said once we were inside. She glanced back at me. "Could you look down here for anything that looks like mine just in case?"

"Of course." I tried to make myself sound like the obliging friend whose sole purpose was to help Eve through this.

I turned left and went through the living room. Eve had given me an idea of the layout of the house to save me time I'd otherwise have wasted on opening bathroom doors.

The living room looked like it'd been decorated to make a statement. The flat screen TV mounted on the wall took up so much space that it wouldn't have even been comfortable to watch, like having to sit too close to the screen in a movie theater. The sofa and chairs were the kind that looked nice, but felt like you were trying to sit on a rock.

At the edge of the living room, I found the door that should lead to the basement. I opened the door and flicked on the bare-switch light. Eve had never been down into the basement. Her first night there, she'd opened the door thinking it led to a powder room, and Anthony told her she was an idiot. She remembered thinking he'd over-reacted. At the time, she'd chocked it up to a bad day.

Basements could hold a lot of things people didn't want found—a secret marijuana-growing operation, stolen goods, weapons, or kidnap victims. Any of which could have gotten him killed.

While it didn't seem likely that an insurance salesman would be involved in anything like that, some of the best criminals hid in plain sight.

The light that came on when I flicked the switch was dim and yellow. The stairs were bare wood, and the walls were cement.

I stepped onto the staircase, and it shifted underneath me. The wood groaned.

A pulse of blood ripped through me, and I leaped backward. I turned on the flashlight on my phone and directed the light at the stairs. Most of the steps were cracked and rotting. A couple were even missing.

Unless there was another way in, it didn't look like the base-ment was used at all. I shone my flashlight into the parts I could see from my spot in the doorway. The windows were high up in the walls, indicating that the basement was mostly underground.

Any other entrance would be obvious from the yard, and Eve had said there were only two doors into the house—the front door we'd entered through and the back door that led from the kitchen into the backyard.

I'd wasted five of my minutes on a dead end. He'd likely yelled at Eve because the basement was dangerous and ugly rather than that he was hiding anything there. He seemed like a man who valued appearances.

Where was my next best option? Eve said he often threw parties. He wouldn't likely leave anything incriminating in the main portion of the house.

Since Eve stayed over, that crossed off the bedroom. He wouldn't risk her stumbling onto something since he'd put effort into keeping her out of the house when he wasn't around.

That left the office.

I passed by the stairs leading up to the second level.

"It should have been right here." Eve's voice floated down the stairs, high-pitched and too rapid-fire. She'd have never survived as a spy. "Did you move anything last time you were here to clean?"

That sounded like Eve was already having to stall for time.

I picked up my pace and found the office at the end of the hall, right where Eve said it would be.

His desk sat empty, a bare space in the middle showing where his computer must have sat. The police had taken it. The drawers for his file cabinet hung open as well, the files gone.

We might have been naïve to think the police would have overlooked something.

I'd use what time I had left searching anyway.

I pulled open his desk drawers. Only office supplies. Just to be sure, I felt the dimensions. Then I felt silly. False bottom drawers were something that really only existed on TV and in movies. You couldn't go to an office supply store or a furniture store and request a desk with secret drawers, and this desk definitely looked like it came from a box store.

Think. I had to think. And pay attention.

There weren't any pictures on the wall, so that meant no hidden safe. Even if there had been, Eve wouldn't have had the code.

A wireless phone handset rested on the desk, but I hadn't seen the base anywhere in the rooms I'd passed through. Maybe he was vain enough that he didn't want anyone seeing a slightly unsightly phone base?

If that were the case, the police could have overlooked it, thinking he only used a cell phone the way so many people did anymore.

Anthony would have still needed to be able to access the phone base to charge the handset and check for messages.

I opened the office closet. The shelves inside held a printer, stacks of paper, and backup boxes of ink.

A small black antenna peeked just over the top of the ink boxes.

I shoved them aside. The phone base stared back at me, the answering machine light blinking.

Footsteps came down the stairs.

"I just need to check the kitchen," Eve said, much too loudly for an inside voice. "I know it sounds silly, but I left my favorite cheese grater here."

I cringed. That didn't sound suspicious *at all*.

I pressed the button on the answering machine.

"You have four new messages," an automated voice said. "First new message."

The first two calls were hang-ups. The third was from his doctor's office, reminding him that he was due for his physical. He wouldn't need that anymore.

This had been a pipe dream. What did I think I was actually going to find on his answering machine, a sobbing confession and apology from his murderer?

"Final message," the automated voice said, and gave the date as the Thursday before the sandcastle competition.

According to Detective Strobel, Anthony died sometime in the night between Friday and Saturday, when I'd been parked next to the beach. The fact that he hadn't checked his message between Thursday and then meant that he must have been either involved in something that distracted him so much that he forgot or the people who killed him had already kidnapped him at that point.

A woman's voice came through the machine. The reception

was bad, cutting out every few words, but her tone was sharp and angry.

"…can't do this to people…you'd better…"

That sounded like a threat. I yanked my phone out of my pocket, flipped to the video feature, and hit record. It was quicker than going to the feature where I could record dictated notes.

The message was almost over. I only caught the last few words. "You'll regret it."

7

*E*ve waved to the cleaning woman as she drove away and then slumped against the side of her car like all her bones suddenly melted. "Please tell me you found something. That was worse than public speaking back in grade school. I can't do that again."

I motioned that we should climb into her car. Anthony's street was empty for now, but I didn't think I should play the snippet of message if there was a chance of someone overhearing.

We both slid inside.

I pulled out my phone. "I found an angry message on his machine. I think it could be someone he fired."

I pressed play and the three words came out loud in the confines of the car.

Eve frowned. "That's it?"

"There was more, but this was all I had time to record." Eve and the cleaning woman had showed up at the office door before I could play it again. I'd had to make up something about finding Eve's favorite stapler just to keep the cleaning woman from becoming suspicious.

Though, in hindsight, that might have sounded more fishy than if I'd simply said I hadn't found anything of Eve's in the office. Eve already had the "favorite cheese grater" in her arms, and a missing favorite stapler might have been going a touch far,

I told Eve the rest of what the message said.

"Play it again," Eve said.

I played it again. Then another time.

Her bottom lip sucked in between her teeth so deeply that it looked like she didn't have one. "I think I recognize the voice. One more time just to be sure."

I did.

Eve stopped chewing her lip. "It sounds like Harper. She used to work at Rigman and Associates, but she quit a month ago."

When Eve thought she recognized the voice, I'd expected it to be someone Anthony fired. The message was angry, and the bits I'd been able to catch sounded like something a person wrongfully let go might say.

What reason would a woman who quit have to be that angry with Anthony?

"Do you know why she quit?"

Eve shook her head. "She was there one day and gone the

next. I only know she quit rather than being fired because Mr. Green, my other boss, told me."

Most jobs asked employees to give at least two weeks' notice if they wanted to quit. That she'd left so quickly could point to a bigger issue behind why she'd left. Maybe Anthony asked her to do something unethical, or he tried to pressure her into sleeping with him. Either of those could be a motive for her to quit, though they wouldn't explain the angry message.

"We need to talk to her."

"I never had to call her outside of work." Eve started the car and pulled away from Anthony's house, where we'd been sitting for far too long. "Mr. Green should still have her contact information, though. I can try the forgotten items story one more time and say she left something behind."

As I was closing up my truck the next day, my phone rang, and the picture I'd taken of Janie shooting Dan with a garden hose flashed onto my screen. The voice on the other end when I answered definitely wasn't Dan's.

"They're here!" Janie squealed in my ear. "Auntie Claire says you can come over and show us how they work."

"You're supposed to *ask* her if she wants to come over," Claire said in the background. "It's not polite to tell a grown-up what to do."

Even as she lectured Janie on manners, I could hear an undertone of excitement in Claire's voice too. She tried not to show it, but she seemed interested in my business.

The *they* had to be my Russian piping tips. They'd been trending all over social media just after I bought my truck, but I hadn't had the money or the mailing address to order some. I couldn't even open a PO box since the post office required identification.

About a month ago, Janie asked me to show her how some of my different piping tips worked, which resulted in us both eating way too many cupcakes, but also in me mentioning the Russian piping tips in passing. Janie begged me to buy some and send them to her house, so she could be there when I opened them and tried them out.

It gave me the perfect solution to how to order a set without telling them I didn't have my own mailing address.

The new piping tips had arrived in perfect timing. If they looked as good in real life as online, they'd make prepping for this weekend's rescheduled sandcastle competition much easier.

I had a test batch of chocolate zucchini cupcakes in my fridge that would be perfect for testing out the tips. All we'd need was the buttercream. "Set out some unsalted butter. I'll be there in fifteen minutes."

By the time Dan walked in the door, we'd covered the cupcakes I'd already made in multi-colored daisies, roses, and tulips thanks to the Russian piping tips and had another batch of vanilla cupcakes fresh from the oven because we were having too much fun to stop. Claire was almost more awed by putting two colors of icing into a single piping bag, squeezing, and having a fully formed flower come out than Janie was. Her first couple of attempts had been a bit of a disaster, but she hadn't given up.

Claire was bent over the last cupcake, her tongue peeking out between her teeth when Dan walked in.

Her head shot up. "You're home early."

One side of Dan's mouth lifted, and he made a show of looking at his watch. "Nope. Right when I thought I'd be."

The piping bag drooped in Claire's hand. She practically tossed it at me. "I haven't even started supper yet, and we can't just eat cupcakes." She plucked Janie off the counter where she'd been perched and set her on the floor. "Go wash the icing off your face."

"Don't show Daddy the cupcakes until I'm back," Janie said, and at Claire's glare added, "Please."

Dan looked around the kitchen. We'd hauled my heavy stand mixer in from my truck because I insisted it made the best buttercream, and the counter and island were dusted with the icing sugar that clouded out of the mixer when Janie turned it on too high, too fast. We had a lot of clean-up before we could even think about supper.

"Why don't I fire up the grill," he said, "and we'll have burgers." He glanced over his shoulder in the direction Janie had gone, then looked back at me. "While we have a minute, I wanted to warn you that an officer might be coming to talk to you about the dead body found at the sandcastle competition."

The fact that he felt he had to specify which dead body spoke to how we'd met. "A Detective Strobel came to my truck this week. He basically gave me the don't-leave-town talk."

No need to tell him that Eve also came to my truck and asked me not to tell the detective what I knew. Dan was as suspicious as I was, though for different reasons. If I told him about Eve, he'd think she was guilty.

Dan looked longingly at the kitchen chairs as if he'd like to sit but instead he moved to the freezer and pulled out a box of frozen burgers. "You're on his persons of interest list."

Dan said it so casually, like it shouldn't make me want to instantly skip town. I watched his profile while he separated burgers with a butter knife.

Maybe casual wasn't the right way to describe his tone. Confident fit better. Unlike last time I'd been too close to a murder victim, he didn't suspect me. In fact, he knew I wouldn't have killed someone.

I sank down into the nearest chair. He had confidence in me.

He gave me that smile that crinkled his eyes a little at the corners. "It's mainly because the body was found so near your truck, and there weren't any drag marks or vehicle tracks onto the sand."

I'd forgotten that detail. The area where Anthony's body had been buried had been smoothed out and cordoned off for the integrity of the competition. When I first opened my truck's flap in the morning, the sand was pristine. The first footprints on it were from the team who'd been assigned to the area. Whoever killed Anthony must have smoothed the sand after burying him. "That sounds like it would make Detective Strobel suspect me even more. I should have heard or seen something. Especially if the killer took the time to return the sand to its original condition afterward."

Dan didn't ask me why I hadn't heard anything. He simply nodded. My chest suddenly felt too small to hold my heart, like when the Grinch's heart grew from being two sizes too small.

"I can't give you any real details, but I'll let you know if we need to think about hiring you a lawyer. Right now, Strobel has someone he thinks is a much more likely suspect. He thinks he'll be making an arrest soon."

The happy bubble in my chest popped. Eve. It had to be Eve. I couldn't tell her what Dan told me without violating his confidence, but as soon as I had a minute, I'd text her to suggest she get the contact information for the woman who quit ASAP.

Claire finished wiping down the counter and tossed the cloth into the sink. "You're not working the case?"

"Can't. I have a personal relationship with Isabel, so it's a conflict of interest." He held the plate full of burgers up in my direction. "One or two?"

I could barely squeak out that I'd take one. I knew Dan meant that he was my friend and not that he and I were anything more. I couldn't be anything more with anyone. I was still married to Jarrod, and I didn't have a way out of our marriage without giving away my location. I wasn't even sure I wanted to be romantically involved with anyone again.

But belonging to someone in even a platonic way...I hadn't had that in so long. I hadn't realized the gaping hole I'd been carrying around inside until Dan's words filled a little corner of it.

He publicly claimed me as a friend. Not just to me. He'd called me a friend privately months ago. Now he'd told his superiors and co-workers that I was his friend. I was someone to him.

I couldn't lose that. Not for anything.

If for no other reason than that I couldn't allow Detective Strobel to jeopardize what I had by eventually making Dan doubt me, I needed to figure out who'd really killed Anthony Rigman.

8

I'd made too many cupcakes this time. I knew it before ten in the morning.

The crowd at the rescheduled sandcastle-building competition was two-thirds of what it'd been shaping up to be the first time. The competitors had also dropped by half. Many of them had probably come from out of town and couldn't travel back for a second weekend. That could explain the smaller crowd too. Some of the missing spectators were likely friends or family of the competitors who'd dropped out.

Since the competition had been rescheduled, a lot of people probably didn't even realize it was on this weekend. Or they'd shown up the last time after everything had closed down and didn't want to be tricked into a similar situation again.

Whatever the reasons, this wasn't going to be nearly as good a day financially as I'd hoped for. If I wasn't able to sell everything I'd made, I'd have to reduce the price and sell them as day-olds or turn them into cake pops. Neither was ideal. The best return on investment always came from fresh sales.

As much as I needed the mobility and independence of running my business out of a food truck rather than a store front, at times like this, I wished I could set down roots with my business too. I wouldn't be nearly as dependent on events and weather and all the other factors I faced if I had a physical location where people could always find me.

A waving arm in my peripheral vision caught my attention. I handed cupcakes to the last two customers who were lined up and turned in the direction of the gesticulating. Eve strode toward my truck, her sandals snapping on the wooden board-walk, a floppy hat and sunglasses protecting her from the sun. Apparently having the Rigman in Rigman & Associates turn up dead at the sandcastle competition hadn't stopped the company from making use of the booth they'd reserved.

"Why aren't you wearing sunglasses?" Eve said as soon as she was close enough for me to hear her. "You're going to get premature squint wrinkles."

I'd never heard of such a thing as premature squint wrinkles before. In fact, I'd never thought about sunglasses as a way to protect my appearance. They'd always been about improving my ability to see. "My pair broke, and I haven't replaced them yet. I wanted to save up for something a bit better than the dollar store pair I had."

And, truth be told, I'd spent what I planned to spend on sunglasses on the Russian piping tips. Eve didn't need to know that. She didn't need to know that I had to make decisions like that.

Eve lifted up on her tiptoes so that more of her showed over the top of my truck's order window. "You won't believe who was assigned to work the booth with me this weekend."

For a breath, I thought she was going to say Anthony and that no one had been assigned to replace him. Except she was smiling like it was a good thing, so that couldn't be the case. Eve might be conflicted about Anthony's death, but she wasn't heartless to the loss of a human life. I had a feeling that once she wasn't a suspect anymore, grief would hit her harder than it was now. As twisted as it was, there was a part of me that would mourn Jarrod if he died. Or, at least, I'd mourn the man I'd wanted him to be.

"Who?" I asked, since it was clear that's what she was waiting for.

"The woman whose voice I recognized on that message on Anthony's machine. Mr. Green hired her back. He thought we'd been a person short now that Anthony's" –her voice stuttered as if she'd realized that the best word to finish the sentence was *dead*– "gone."

If she'd agreed to come back to work for Rigman & Associates that quickly, it added fuel to our theory that Anthony might have been the reason she quit in the first place. Now that she'd been re-hired, she had a double motive for wanting Anthony dead. Because she'd quit rather than being fired, the police probably weren't investigating her either.

Eve bounced twice. "When I went to Mr. Green to get her phone number, he said she'd be here today. I didn't even have to give him our excuse of needing to return some of her stuff."

"Did she call to get her job back after the news that Anthony died or did your other boss call her?"

Who initiated the re-hire could be important. If she called to get her job back, we'd have the start of a motive, especially given how angry she sounded on the message.

Eve shrugged. "But you should come with me to ask her. You're better at all this cloak-and-dagger stuff than I am. She thinks I'm getting cupcakes right now." Eve handed me enough cash for two cupcakes. "I can tell her I brought you back to meet her because I'm hoping you'll cater our summer barbecue, and I want Harper's help in backing you as a replacement to Mr. Green. The caterer we've always hired recently quit, so she'll believe it."

Eve gave me the whole pitch without seeming to need to breathe. I was continually awed at how many words she managed to pack into a single sentence.

I glanced outside my truck. No one appeared to be heading my way. Most people had set up their umbrellas and beach chairs in the spectator areas next to their favored competitors. Any "lunch rush" wouldn't happen for at least another thirty minutes.

I scribbled *back at 11:00* on a piece of paper and stuck it to the side of my truck's ordering window. "Lead the way."

Harper was leaning back in her chair at the booth when we arrived, looking like she wished she could either put her feet up on the table or take a nap. Their booth was more deserted than my truck at present. Honestly, I wasn't sure why an insurance company would even want space at an event like this unless it was for name recognition. No one wanted to discuss insurance policies at the beach. It was like the mayor who'd been here the first weekend. I doubted anyone changed their mind about whom to vote for because they gave them a calendar or free miniature chocolate bar.

She looked up as we approached, probably alerted by the sound of Eve's clapping shoes. "Did you get me the weirdest kind she had?"

Her gaze landed on me, and her expression shifted slightly— wider eyes and a blush creeping over her caramel-colored cheeks. She obviously thought I was a potential customer, and her statement would be viewed as unprofessional.

I held out my hand quickly. "I'm Isabel. I run How Sweet It Is Cupcake Truck."

"And she's a friend of mine." Eve took the chair next to Harper, and handed her one of the cupcakes. "Peanut butter and jelly. Trust me, it's amazing."

My brain couldn't quite wrap itself around the fact that Eve had called me a friend. We barely knew each other. Then again, maybe that was part of the act. She didn't want Harper to know that we'd been thrown into a strange acquaintance thanks to Anthony's murder. Or maybe I simply made friends more slowly than was normal.

"I want to convince Mr. Green to hire Isabel to cater the annual barbecue." Eve gave a smile whose wattage rivaled the sun. "I need to bring you over to my side, so I have an ally."

Harper took a bite of the PB&J cupcake, and her eyes rolled back in her head. "You've got one. I didn't think they were going to still have the barbecue, though. Not since someone rid the world of Anthony." Her gaze snapped up to Eve as if she just realized that she'd implied that it was a good thing Eve's boyfriend was dead. "I didn't mean..." She heaved a sigh. "Actually I did mean it. We'll all be better off without him, including you."

She called Anthony a few choice words to emphasize her point.

If Harper had killed Anthony, she wasn't exactly being subtle about her dislike for him. If it were me, I'd be trying to act like I hadn't hated him. Though her openness could be the best way to hide. No one would suspect a murderer to be so open about their dislike out of fear of shining a spotlight on themselves.

"The barbecue's still on," Eve said, but her voice was two sizes too small for her body.

"Good." Harper stuffed the rest of the cupcake into her

mouth and gave a happy little moan. "We shouldn't be punished because someone finally refused to put up with him anymore."

Jarrod used to tell me stories about his interrogation of suspects. He liked to say that if you gave a suspect enough verbal rope, they'd hang themselves. I leaned a hip against their booth, trying to look casual. "You sound like you didn't like him."

Harper rolled her eyes again, but this time the move signaled the opposite of what it had before. "The man was a sexist and a racist. He wanted me to wear short skirts and low cut blouses because he thought the male customers wouldn't ask too many questions if I flashed them a little skin, but he wouldn't let me wear my hair down."

Harper had her hair pulled back into a ponytail, but the part that hung loose out of the hair tie had beautiful, voluminous corkscrew curls.

My throat tightened. I knew what it was like to have someone else control my appearance, but I didn't know what it must be like to have someone attack my appearance in a way that they wouldn't if I was a different race. Sometimes it was hard enough being a woman in this world, let alone a woman of color where people would judge her for both her gender and her skin tone without knowing anything else about her.

Eve looked a little like she'd been slapped. "I wear my hair down all the time."

Harper's lips softened slightly around the corners. She must have thought that everyone at the office knew how Anthony was treating her and just hadn't been willing to stand up to him. Given what I knew of Eve's relationship with Anthony, she might not have been brave enough to stand up to him, but at least she hadn't known.

"He said my hair was 'too messy'." Harper put the last two words in air quotes. "And I needed to either have it straightened or wear it back." She shook her head in a way that said this wasn't the first time she'd experienced a micro-aggression, but that it never stopped hurting, and she couldn't quite understand it no matter how often it happened. "I only quit because of the environment he created, and then he made sure I couldn't find another job."

"He refused to give you a reference?" Eve asked before I could gather my thoughts.

Her voice had the tone of someone whose whole worldview had been shattered. With all she knew of Anthony, with how he'd treated her, she could still be surprised that he'd do what he'd done to Harper.

Or perhaps she didn't realize that things like that actually still happened to anyone. She could have thought that the way Anthony treated her was an isolated event because they were dating.

"He gave me a poor reference, which is worse. I didn't even realize it until I'd interviewed for three jobs, and the last place told me I would have gotten the position had it not been for my references."

"Mr. Green would have given you a great reference." The look on Eve's face said she took some responsibility for what had happened, as if it might have made some difference if she'd stood up to Anthony sooner. "He didn't even wait a week to hire you back."

Harper's face changed, softened like she didn't know whether to be hurt or grateful. "Mr. Green wouldn't give me a reference at all. He hired me back as a form of penance. I called him as soon as I heard about Anthony."

Eve put a hand to her forehead, pushing her hat back. "That doesn't sound like him. I don't understand." She held her hand up quickly. "Not that I'm doubting you or trying to downplay it. I just don't understand."

Harper shook her head. "I went in to talk to him personally, and he refused without giving me a reason. He looked like he wanted to cry when he did it." She clenched her jaw, making a muscle jump in her cheek. "I passed Anthony on my way out, and he smirked at me. He might have only been the co-owner, but he controlled everything and everyone in the office."

Her voice wasn't even spiteful. She spoke as if Anthony's iron rule was a well-known fact.

Eve's head was bobbing as if she couldn't deny Harper's assessment. They both seemed to have momentarily forgotten I was there. Which was fine. I'd always been better at observing before coming to a conclusion.

My conclusion in this case was that Harper was a perfect

suspect. Her message on Anthony's answering machine made complete sense in context. He'd refused to give her a good reference, and he'd blocked her other boss from supplying her with a reference. In the current job market, good references mattered more than experience. You couldn't get a job that paid higher than minimum wage without them.

She must have been calling to tell Anthony that he couldn't keep destroying her life simply because she'd refused to work for him. She'd told him he'd regret it.

The problem was I didn't want Harper to have killed Anthony any more than I wanted Eve to have killed Anthony. She'd been treated poorly, and he'd continued to persecute her even once he wasn't her boss anymore. What he'd done wasn't fair.

But if she'd killed him, I couldn't protect her at my expense or at Eve's expense either. As soon as I could get away, I'd call Dan and let him decide what to do with the information.

9

Summer in Michigan wasn't supposed to be hot enough that I couldn't make a proper buttercream or batch of cupcakes.

I pressed my clean thumb into the butter again to see if it had warmed up to the perfect consistency yet. Since the weather grew hot, I hadn't been able to simply leave my butter in the shelves so that it'd always be room temperature and ready to use. Unless I had the air conditioning on in my truck, "room temperature" butter ended up solid but shiny and greasy looking—a sign that it was too soft and wouldn't whip up properly—or completely melted, which I couldn't use at all unless I wanted to bake a batch of chewy chocolate chip cookies.

This wouldn't have been a problem if I'd had somewhere else to bake the cupcakes. But, as the old saying went, if wishes were horses…

My cell phone vibrated across the countertop, and I scooped it up. Watched butter didn't soften any quicker than watching a pot of water made it boil faster.

Dan name flashed on my screen. I swiped my finger across to answer.

I'd called him last weekend with everything I'd learned about Harper as soon as I got another break in customers. I hadn't been completely honest with him about how I came by the information. What I'd said was that I was near Rigman & Associates booth at the sandcastle competition, and I'd overheard them talking. Technically, it was true. I had been standing next to the booth listening. I'd just left out the part where Eve invited me there in the hope that we'd get some good information out of Harper.

Once we'd spoken to her, Eve hadn't looked any more excited than I was to think Harper might be the murderer. Assuming the worst of a person you barely knew was easy. Still wanting that person to turn out to be a murderer once you'd met them and heard their story was a lot harder.

"I passed the name you gave me along to Detective Strobel," Dan said. "I had to come at it sideways since he's not known for liking other detectives meddling in his cases without invitation."

I poked the stick of butter again just to be sure. I couldn't quite make the easy indentation I needed. If I used it before I could easily leave a thumbprint, my sugar wouldn't be able to aerate my butter properly, and I'd end up with dense cupcakes.

Creating air pockets in the butter was part of the science of baking. Knowing when your butter was at the perfect stage of softness was part of the art.

"Do you think he'll tell you what he finds out?"

Dan's end of the call crackled, and I almost missed what he said. The words I caught were *he did, didn't,* and *pan out.*

I was about to ask him to repeat that when the call cleared.

"Harper Castle was out of town," Dan was saying, "staying with her parents in Detroit for a job interview, the weekend of the original sandcastle competition. She left on Thursday night because the interview was on Friday. Her parents and the company she was interviewing with confirmed her alibi."

The job interview explained her angry call to Anthony. If she'd gone out of town for an interview, she was getting desperate for a job. She knew that if the interview went well, her potential employer would call her references. That could have been a motive. With Anthony gone, Mr. Green would have likely given her a good reference.

All that aside, she hadn't had the opportunity to kill him. In light of her interview, her phone call actually spoke to her innocence, even if she had been in town during the window of opportunity. She'd called to threaten him to give her an honest reference. Her interview was on Friday. Reference checks wouldn't have happened until the following week at the earliest. By then, Anthony was dead. Unless Harper's thinking was completely convoluted, it wouldn't make sense for her to call him about references and then kill him before she could find out if he gave her a good reference or a bad one.

A tangled knot of relief and panic flooded through me. They wouldn't be arresting Harper. But that meant Eve and I were still the primary suspects. I didn't know whether I should respond to what Dan told me with *that's good* for Harper's sake or with *that's too bad* for Eve and me.

"Are you worrying about this case?" Dan asked, his voice gentle. "I've been trying to figure out why else you would've been hanging around the Rigman Insurance booth when you should have been manning your truck."

I leaned back against my fridge. I knew I wasn't that transparent. I'd learned not to be. So either Dan was starting to know me better than I realized, or he was using the skills that had served him well when he'd been an undercover detective.

"Yes," I said.

The word came out before I could consider whether honesty was the best policy in this case. Maybe he would think I was worried because I'd had something to do with it after all. I couldn't remember if I'd told him that I'd met the dead man or not.

I didn't want to give him any reason to doubt me and consider restricting my access to Janie. I'd even picked her up from school a couple of times before summer break, which meant he'd added me to the list of safe people the school could release Janie to. Having someone trust me that way meant more than I could ever explain.

"You don't need to worry. Detective Strobel's…hard to work with, but he's honest." A gust of wind rustled across the speaker on Dan's cell phone. He must have gone outside to call me. "He won't plant evidence. He won't arrest someone with shaky evidence just to close his case."

He's not like Jarrod.

I could almost hear Dan thinking the words even though he didn't seem to want to say them. Detective Strobel wouldn't arrest me without conclusive evidence, and he would never have conclusive evidence because I hadn't killed Anthony.

A warm little bubble formed in my stomach, making me want to smile. Not only had Dan guessed that I was worried, but he'd taken the time to reassure me again that he knew I hadn't murdered anyone.

What had I done to deserve that kind of a friend?

"Thank you." I whispered the words so softly that I wasn't sure if he would be able to hear them or if I'd have to clear my throat and try again.

"You're welcome," he said. "You can return the favor next time Janie needs to bring something to a party or bake sale at school."

I grinned wide enough that my cheeks hurt. "That's a deal."

In fact, it was one where I benefited all around.

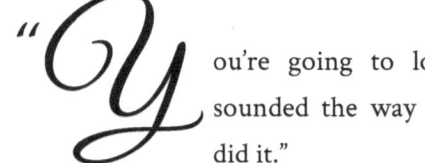"ou're going to love me forever." Eve's voice sounded the way champagne bubbles looked. "I did it."

I put my phone on speaker and propped it up so that I could continue forming the buttercream roses for my brown butter cupcakes.

The more I got to know Eve, the more her energy level and enthusiasm reminded me of a squirrel or a puppy. She hadn't seemed so exuberant the times she'd come to my cupcake truck. Granted, buying a cupcake didn't show anything about a person except whether they were adventurous or a creature of habit, but I couldn't help but think this was also a result of Anthony being gone from her life.

As great as it was for her personally, it wasn't good for her appearance of guilt. If Detective Strobel saw that she was happier now than before, the real murderer would have to confess to take Eve out of Number One Suspect spot.

Had Detective Strobel heard her right now, he might have even taken her words as a confession. Even with her newfound freedom, I doubted Eve would sound so jubilant had she decided to confess to murder. Especially to me, since I'd been trying to help prove that we were both innocent.

"You did it," I said cautiously.

"I got you the job catering our annual company barbecue."

Her tone said it should have been obvious. I hadn't realized she was serious about trying to get me a gig. I thought that was a ruse to explain why she'd brought me to meet Harper.

"Harper raved about your cupcakes so much when we went back into the office on Monday that the few holdouts who I haven't convinced to eat cupcakes for lunch changed their mind."

Catering the entire barbecue wasn't quite the same as supplying cupcakes for dessert. "Sweet and savory?"

"Of course. That's what the caterer we've always hired up to this point did so everyone will be expecting it."

I looped the buttercream to form the final petal and placed the tiny rose into the fridge. I'd found that the best way to handled buttercream flowers was to create them ahead of time on small slips of parchment paper. I simply snipped the parchment paper base off when I was ready to use them, and the flowers were less likely to be damaged than if I placed them right on the cupcakes and then had to store the decorated version.

As much as I appreciated Eve actually putting me forward for the catering job, I wasn't a savory chef. Or, more precisely, I didn't have a tried and tested set of recipes and routines ready to go. My skills were rusty.

And yet, I could always use the money and the referrals that came from doing an event like that. Maybe I could handle it if it wasn't too big an event. "How many people come and what's the date?"

The number of people and date Eve gave me made me squirt a dollop of icing off the side of my parchment paper and ruin the flower I'd been working on. When I'd tentatively prayed, asking God for more work, I hadn't meant *please drop lots of jobs into my lap on short notice.* I couldn't be ready to cater that size of an event in that amount of time. Not alone anyway. I'd either have to work with another food truck, halving my profit, or get help with the prep work.

I had no idea Rigman & Associates was such a big firm.

Something niggled at the back of my mind. I set aside my piping bag so that my brain wouldn't be trying to talk, think, and work at the same time.

The fully formed thought pinged to the front. If this was such a lucrative event, why had the caterer who'd been working the event for years suddenly quit?

"I don't want you to think I'm not grateful—"

"Don't say no." I could almost see Eve gripping her phone

and rising up onto her tip toes. "This is a great opportunity to grow your business. Trust me, I know. I'm in marketing."

Eve probably was able to sell a lot of things—ideas included—simply by the force of her excitement.

"I'm just wondering why the previous caterer quit. Was there a problem with payment or unreasonable requests? My margins not large enough to handle something like that."

"Mr. Green is fastidious about doing the right thing." Eve's voice was so confident it was hard to doubt anything she said. "I think it was a personality conflict between the catering service and Anthony."

That I could believe. The man seemed to have a "personal conflict" with almost everyone he met.

Eve quoted the amount Rigman & Associates was willing to pay.

It was probably foolish of me to consider accepting, but Janie's birthday was coming up. I wanted to be able to do more than bake her birthday cake as my present.

"And if that wasn't enough to sway you," Eve continued, clearly interpreting my hesitation as what it was, "it'll be a chance for us to figure out who else in the company might have had a reason to kill Anthony. There's always alcohol, and people get a little tipsy and talk too much. Trust me, no one hated Anthony as much as the people working for him. It's out best chance."

Eve was right. Based on what Dan had said, I got the impression that Eve was still at the top of Detective Strobel's list and I wasn't far behind. Even though he wouldn't be able to find concrete evidence against us, that didn't mean one of us wouldn't end up arrested. Strobel might be the kind of man Dan said he was. But he had superiors. Superiors who would want the case closed eventually and might not have the same qualms about arresting someone based on circumstantial evidence as Strobel did.

As long as Eve and I were under investigation, we had to keep investigating, and her company's barbecue was the best place to talk to and eavesdrop on people who'd had to work with Anthony and might—like Harper—have had reasons to want him dead.

11

This was one conversation with Claire that I wanted to have in person. I hadn't even had the courage to call her first and ask if I could come over. I might lose my nerve if she said no. I'd barely been able to sleep last night rehearsing over and over how I'd ask her to help me cater the event and let me use her freezer to store the prepared food.

By the time I turned onto her street, I was almost hoping she wouldn't be home so that I could put it off. She might not want to help, even though she'd told me she was the one who taught Dan how to cook. Then I'd have to try to partner with another food truck, and it would cost me at least half my profit.

She might also see through my lie about why I couldn't store all the food we needed to prepare in advance at my own place. If I couldn't use her freezer, I'd have to give up the job entirely.

I slowed to a stop in front of Claire's house. If possible, her gardens were even more perfectly manicured than they had been before. The purples and yellows of the flowers looked like they'd been carefully selected to enhance each other when side by side, and her lawn didn't have a single dandelion or other weed.

There was also a FOR SALE sign out front with the name and phone number of a local Realtor on it.

Claire hadn't mentioned that she was trying to sell her house.

I rested my hand on the gear shift. Maybe this was stupid. Clearly I didn't know Claire. She didn't feel comfortable sharing things with me. Why would she be willing to help me? Catering this event was a big ask. It was hours of preparation, not to mention the time spent at the event itself. I planned to offer to pay her, of course, but if she was preparing to move, she might not even have time. This was a lot more than her offer to help me sell at big events if I couldn't handle serving a crowd.

I shouldn't have come.

I put my truck back into drive, but Claire's front door opened before I could pull away from the curb. She made a *come here* motion with her hand.

She probably couldn't see my face. I could pretend I hadn't seen her.

The memory of her expression when she'd been trying to solve my financial problems popped into my head. She'd wanted to help me then. Not in the same way, but perhaps it showed that I shouldn't cross her off without trying.

I shifted my truck back into park and turned it off.

Claire was already down her front steps, her shoulders tense and a frown on her face. "Are you alright?"

"No...err, yes."

Claire stopped and planted her hands on her hips.

Is this what it would have been like to have a mom or an older sister? My dad had been the best dad in the world, but he hadn't known how to be both a mom and a dad for me. I hadn't known what I was missing when I was young. It wasn't until I was in my late teens and watching other girls with their moms that I realized.

Claire's expression said *go on, I'm waiting.*

"I was hired for a catering job, but it's sweet and savory, and it's too much for me to handle on my own."

I explained everything Eve had told me about the event, leaving out the part where I'd accepted in order to check out possible suspects for Anthony's murder.

"I was hoping you'd help," I finished lamely. "I'd pay you."

Heat burned my neck and cheeks worse than if I'd been out all day without sunscreen. Claire probably didn't need my money. She might even be insulted. But I couldn't presume on our tentative relationship enough to ask for her help without offering anything at all.

"Okay," Claire said and turned back toward the house as if she expected me to follow her.

So I did.

Claire glanced back at me over her shoulder. "What's the counter space like at your apartment?"

My feet felt like they'd grown too sizes too large for my body, leaving me clumsy. *You prepared for this*, I reminded myself. "Tiny. Non-existent really." I used everything I'd learned from living with Jarrod not to blurt the words out frantically and give away my lie. Or perhaps it wasn't a lie. The counters in my apartment were non-existent. Literally. Since there was no apartment. "We'd be more comfortable working here if you're alright with that. My freezer's too small too for everything we'll need to store anyway. I only have that kind that's a drawer below the fridge."

In for a lie penny, in for a lie pound.

"I have an old one in the garage that I can hook back up," she said. "I was going to try to sell it, but that can wait a couple more weeks."

Claire was being surprisingly obliging.

The part of me that had learned the hard way to distrust everything that seemed too good to be true tried to tell me that Claire must have an ulterior motive. I just couldn't come up with what that might be.

And I couldn't help but remember what Dan had said about her. That she was a good person. That she'd warm up to me.

Maybe this was Claire warm. Warm was relative, right? If I'd just finished a popsicle, even a glass of water full of ice might seem warm.

Claire directed me to sit on her living room couch. I'd been in this room once before, when Dan brought me to tell Claire that I suspected her of killing her grandfather. It'd had a few boxes in it then, remnants of her husband's exodus. The boxes seemed to have multiplied rather than diminishing since then. The new boxes were neatly labeled. Claire's house didn't have a sold sign on it yet, but she was clearly anticipating the moment when it did.

Claire came back out with a recipe box, the kind where you wrote down a recipe on a cue card and slid it into the correct category. She sat beside me and pulled out a stack of cards. "These are the appetizers and finger foods I used to use when I threw dinner parties with Mike. He never complained so you know they must be good."

Claire's expression turned wry.

According the Dan, Claire's husband had moved out months ago to share an apartment with the woman he cheated on Claire with. He still hadn't given Claire a divorce. For months, he'd even come back to take a box of his stuff at a time. Dan had finally convinced Claire to allow him to haul all of Mike's remaining things out to the curb and then call him to say they were there waiting for him. The way Dan told the story, Mike pounded on the door but had backed off when Dan answered rather than Claire.

I'd gotten the impression Mike was hard to please, to put it mildly.

Claire's cell phone rang. She handed me the cards. "No pictures, but I'm sure you can imagine them from the descriptions."

She slid her finger across the screen and mouthed the words *It's Dan* to me.

I started sorting through Claire's stack of cards. Dips were out. They were fine at small gatherings, but at large events, no one wanted to deal with communal food. Too many people didn't understand that double dipping was taboo.

She did have some great looking recipes for antipasti bites, pizza sliders, cheese and broccoli quiche, jalapeno poppers, and figs stuffed with goat cheese and wrapped in bacon. Savory wasn't my specialty, but my mouth watered thinking of taste testing some of them.

The fact that I'd been too nervous to eat today probably contributed.

"I hung it on the laundry line to dry." Claire dropped back onto the couch beside me. "I'm here with Isabel now if you want to come get it."

I could hear the deep tenor of his voice on the other side of the phone even though I couldn't hear his words.

"Yes at my house." Claire's voice had a snap to it. "I said I was home, didn't I?"

Dan must have found it hard to believe that Claire and I would be spending time together without him and Janie. I didn't blame him. My dad used to like to watch re-runs of *The Odd*

Couple where one roommate was a slob and the other was OCD about cleanliness. Claire and I weren't as mismatched as that, but we weren't an obvious choice for a friendship either. I still wasn't sure if we were friends.

She disconnected. "Dan's on his way. Janie forgot her bathing suit yesterday when she came to swim."

I hadn't even realized Claire had a pool. That should make her house even easier to sell. If I had a bathing suit myself, I might even find the courage to ask if I could come to swim myself before then. I was on the swim team in high school until my dad got sick and I had to quit.

I showed Claire the appetizers I was considering, and she helped pick out a few more. We created a list of what could be made ahead of time and frozen and what would need to be made no more than twenty-four hours in advance. I added the cupcakes that I'd been thinking about making to the lists.

A knock came at the door, but Claire didn't bother getting up to answer it. She had her eyes narrowed, glaring at the paper, as she jotted timelines down, creating a schedule for how long we had to complete each dish in order to stay on track.

Dan appeared in the doorway. His gaze swept over the detritus of our work covering the coffee table. His look of confusion was so intense that I had to hide a smile behind my hand.

"Are you planning a party?" he asked.

"A job," Claire said without looking up from her work. "I'm helping Isabel cater a barbecue for an insurance company."

Dan's body language changed. I couldn't explain it precisely. The closest I could come in my mind was that before he'd had the loose-joints look of a cat lazing around in the sun. Now those muscles had bunched as if he needed to react to a threat.

"An insurance company?" His voice was too casual. "Which one?"

Claire tapped her pen against her lips, her eyes still focused on the pages. "Rigman and Associates."

Dan's head swiveled in my direction. "I've heard of them."

His gaze felt like it was digging through my defenses, right into my brain. He suspected.

He smiled, but it stayed on his lips. "Isabel, can I talk to you in the kitchen for a minute? That way we won't disturb Claire's concentration as she works."

I rose slowly to my feet. Claire didn't even acknowledge me leaving. When it came to planning and organizing, she seemed to go into her own little world.

Dan closed the kitchen door once we were both inside. He leaned back against the counter, his arms crossed over his chest. He looked so casual that I almost thought I'd been wrong. Almost.

Dan had been an undercover police officer before his brother died, and he adopted Janie. He knew how to keep everything off his features and out of his voice that he didn't want there.

My body tensed, every muscle feeling as stiff as my bones. He had to be angry. I could see it from his perspective. I'd been sneaking around. Or, at the very least, I planned to.

"Please tell me this job is completely about the money and there's no other reason you're catering this event." His voice was soft, almost sad.

I hadn't expected that. I'd expected anger and accusations. I'd expected him to jump to conclusions and berate me.

I forced myself to meet Dan's blue eyes. They were as soft as his voice.

Dan, I reminded myself for what felt like the millionth time, *isn't Jarrod.*

I couldn't lie to him. I couldn't make myself confess. I stood there mute, feeling stupid.

Dan ran a hand over his face. He pushed up straight. "If you get caught poking around in this case, it could make you look guilty. You could have come to me instead. I thought we agreed to work as a team."

We had back in May, but I hadn't thought that was an open-ended agreement. "Wasn't that only for your grandfather's case?"

Dan smiled in that way that crinkled his eyes and sent a strange spiral of warmth through my stomach. "You seem to want to keep investigating deaths. Maybe we should make it a permanent agreement."

How did a man who'd been through so much, seen so much, still manage to smile like that? It made me feel hopeful. Like I could have joy too if I was willing to fight for it.

"If you're catering this party to snoop around," Dan said, "I want to be there as one of your employees."

I couldn't stop the return smile that tugged at my lips. "Not only to snoop around."

"It'll make your business look more successful to have more than you and Claire anyway." Dan held out his hand like he'd done the first time. "Do we have a deal?"

I narrowed my eyes and crossed my arms, but I couldn't wipe away the smile. "I didn't want to pay another employee."

Dan kept his hand extended. A less confident man would have lowered it. Dan stayed still, as if he believed without doubting that I'd relent. "You can pay me in cupcakes."

"For how long?"

Something flickered across his face that I couldn't interpret, and his smile drained away from his eyes a little even though it stayed on his lips. "To be determined."

I slid my palm into his and shook. "You're hired."

He gave my hand an extra squeeze before letting go. "Tell me what you've been up to so far."

I filled him in on what Eve and I had uncovered, including confessing the half-truth I'd told him about how I got the information about Harper and Anthony.

The smile fell off of Dan's face completely as I spoke. "Eve got you the catering job too?"

I nodded.

"Did she tell you she's also a suspect?"

I opened my mouth to tell him that she came to me shortly after I'd spoken to the police to ask me not to tell them anything. I realized in time that made her sound guilty. I nodded again instead. "My last partnership investigating a crime went so well that I thought I'd try it again."

The concerned look stayed on his face as if my attempt at flattery slid right off Dan and didn't stick.

He moved a little closer in a way that suggested it was subconscious. "I can't give you the details, but Detective Strobel has good reasons for suspecting her. Promise me you'll be careful."

That strange warm spiral kicked up in my belly again. Maybe I should feel insulted since I was one of the most careful people he'd likely ever meet. Maybe I should try to argue Eve's innocence.

But having someone care about me ripped all those words right out of me, and all I could say was, "I promise."

12

"This is the best one yet." The woman slowly chewed the tiny bite she'd taken of the lemon meringue cupcake, and her eyes slid shut behind glasses that were too big for her face. "How many varieties did you say you brought again?"

Three boys around the age of ten raced past me toward where the three-legged race was about to start, and I stepped aside to give them more room. I didn't want to end up wearing the tray of cupcakes I carried. It'd almost happened twice already today. Weaving through the crowd at the Rigman & Associates annual barbecue felt a bit like trying to find my way through a maze that kept changing. "Six flavors of cupcakes, but we also have appetizers if you're looking for something savory instead of sweet."

"Six!" Her eyes owled open. She chucked the half-finished

lemon meringue cupcake into the nearby trash can and snatched a peanut butter and jelly one from my tray. "I'm going to need room to try them all. Maybe I should have entered that silly potato sack race after all."

Don't stare at the trash can, I admonished myself. She couldn't possibly know how it hurt a baker's soul to see something they'd created tossed away rather than eaten. Not to mention we'd run out early if everyone decided to eat only one bite.

"Flag me down when you have some other varieties with you," the woman was saying. "We should have switched over to you years ago. The other company's desserts tasted like cardboard. I might as well have been eating diet food."

She took one bite from the peanut butter and jelly cupcake, tossed it into the trash with the lemon meringue, and wandered away.

I shuddered. I'd gotten half my payment upfront, and Eve assured me the company would be good to pay me the rest, so at least the woman wasn't throwing away my money. Still...

I turned away and continued weaving through the crowd. I needed to focus not only on doing my official job but on listening for anything that might give us a new lead in Anthony's murder. The serving trays had been Dan's idea. If we were going to eavesdrop on people, we needed to be out among them. If they had to come to us, they'd stop any interesting conversation right about the time we'd be able to hear it.

Anthony's death was fresh enough that it was still a hot topic of conversation, but I hadn't heard anything incriminating or useful yet.

"Have you tried the food?" a man's voice said to the woman he was standing with as I wiggled through the small space behind him between him and the rope that had been put up to cordon off the "open bar."

"They don't have the crab cakes I liked so much." The woman's voice had a pout to it. "I don't know why they switched to someone new this year. We've had the same caterer as long as I've been with the company."

I felt more than saw the man's shoulders shrug. "I don't know, but you should try something. I enjoyed almost everything I've tried." He said it hesitantly like he was afraid of contradicting her.

I didn't know whether to put that conversation in the pro-us category or the con-us. So far, Claire and I seemed to be coming out ahead of the other caterer in how much people were enjoying the food. But there were a few who couldn't seem to understand why the company had decided to mess with a good thing by changing caterers.

The switch after so many years did seem strange. Based on what Eve had said, Rigman & Associates hadn't initiated the change. The caterer had cancelled on them. On short notice no less.

Most caterers wouldn't quit a job that close to the date unless something serious happened. Not only would cancelling an event last minute create a gap in their income, but it would mean a poor review or poor word of mouth. As Anthony had proven, he had no trouble actively seeking to destroy the careers of people who crossed him.

I was probably fishing, but it wouldn't hurt to find out what was behind the caterer quitting. The more I heard people talk about how long the previous caterer had worked the event, the more suspicious I become. They'd worked for Rigman & Associates for years, both their summer cookout and their Christmas party, only to quit so close to Anthony's death. The timing seemed too convenient.

My tray emptied out, and I headed back to my truck to restock. Out of the corner of my eye, I glimpsed Dan also moving through the crowd. Or trying to. A woman in a clingy sundress blocked his path, some sort of brightly colored drink in her hand.

From this distance, it looked like she was flirting with him. I couldn't blame her. Somehow the bubble-gum pink shirts Claire had bought us to wear today made his blue eyes look even bluer.

I focused back on loading up cupcakes. As long as Dan looked like he was actually an employee of How Sweet It Is cupcake truck, I shouldn't care about anything else. Who he flirted with wasn't any of my business. I shouldn't care how blue his eyes were. I was a married woman.

My tray filled with strawberry cheesecake cupcakes and

cookies and cream cupcakes, I headed back into the center of the party. An arm waved above the crowd, and in between the other people, I caught sight of a pair of oversized glasses bobbing toward me.

No way. I couldn't handle watching more of my hard work end up nestled among rotting banana peels and dirty paper plates.

I ducked behind the tiki hut-style building where alcohol was being served.

"Do you think she did it?" The same woman's voice as I'd heard before came from just around the opposite corner. Her words had the tiniest lisp to them now, as if whatever she was drinking wasn't the first she'd had. She might not want to eat my food because I didn't have crab cakes, but she had no qualms about the free liquor.

"Who?" the man's voice responded.

"Eve, obviously. Do you think she killed him?"

The man snorted. "Of course she did. You should have heard the way he ran her down in the creative meeting for the new ads. No one could take that kind of treatment for long."

"Mr. Green should have bought out Rigman's share of the company years ago." Anger and regret mingled in the woman's voice. I couldn't help but notice that she didn't call Anthony *Mr.* Rigman. It was like she couldn't stomach giving him that level of respect even now that he was dead. "If he had, we wouldn't have had so much trouble with turnover, and Eve wouldn't end up spending the next decade or more of her life in prison."

"Maybe she'll hire a good defense attorney." The man's voice was getting softer as if they were walking away. "I'd testify for her if she wanted to argue self-defense or battered woman syndrome or whatever."

The woman made an affirming noise before they were too far away for me to hear any more.

What chance did Eve have if even her co-workers believed her capable of murder? Then again, maybe it was less that they believed her capable of murder. Maybe it was that they thought they would have killed Anthony had they been in her position. No one seemed to condemn her actions if she had done it.

A tiny wriggle of doubt ate at my heart like a worm pushing its way into an already rotting apple. I couldn't let it take hold. Eve said she hadn't done it. I needed to believe her until irrefutable proof showed otherwise. Even more so since it seemed like I was the only one who did believe her.

You're an idiot, Fear hissed in my head. *A gullible idiot.*

"There you are!" a woman shouted before I could decide whether Fear was right this time or not.

I turned around. Big Glasses Woman stood behind me.

"Ooo!" she squealed and grabbed a cupcake in each hand. "Yummy!"

~

I SANK DOWN ONTO DAN'S COUCH, AND HE TOOK THE ARM CHAIR beside me, kicking the footrest out and lacing his hands behind his head. "I need to do more cardio. My feet feel like I ran a marathon."

We'd dropped Claire off at her house, and Dan had invited me back to his place for a cup of my homemade hot chocolate. Janie wouldn't be home yet for another couple hours from her play date with her cousins.

Dan smothered a yawn, and it brought a grin to my face.

Something about catering such a big event left me feeling light, as if my body wasn't tethered to the ground. Light and happy. "Maybe you need better shoes," I said deadpan, even though I couldn't keep the laugh out of my voice.

Maybe it was having worked together today or maybe the giddiness of successfully pulling this event off had all gone to my head, but it suddenly felt safe to tease him.

He sat up slightly. "What's wrong with my shoes?"

He'd been wearing loafers. They were the kind of shoes that looked good with a tie but weren't meant for walking around all day. "Nothing if you're sitting at a desk."

He gave me a mock glare. "I might not be doing undercover work anymore, but I hardly spend my days behind a desk."

I gave him an *uh huh, sure* look, but spoiled it with a smile. My lips just wanted to go up. Despite everything else that was going on, it felt good to have something with my business go so very right. For something in my life to go right.

The memory of the woman in the sundress flirting with Dan flitted across my mind. My smile withered, and the couch suddenly felt hard underneath me. As well as things seemed to be going, I shouldn't get comfortable here. Dan was currently single, but that woman's attention—drunk or not—proved that there were probably plenty of woman who'd like to change his status. When that happened, I wouldn't find the same welcome here.

My Sunday night family dinners would be over. My evenings making us hot chocolate and popcorn and watching movies on the couch with Janie would be over. Him calling me just to chat would be over. Even a very secure woman wouldn't want a quasi-homeless woman with a fake name hanging around as if she were family when she wasn't.

A funny gaping feeling opened up in my chest. It felt like a smaller version of what I felt when I sat by my dad's bed, watching him die. Which was silly of me. Dan would still be my friend, even if the dynamics of that friendship had to change. And I'd never want to stand in the way of Janie having a mother again.

I just didn't want to think about it ahead of time was all. Joking with him brought what I stood to lose to the forefront. We'd come here to compare notes about the day, and we should stick to that. Anything else was like continuing to poke at a bruise and then wondering why it was taking so long to heal.

"Did you learn anything that might help figure out who killed Anthony Rigman?" I asked.

Dan leaned back again, his expression sobering in a mirror to mine. "No one seemed to like him, but the worst I heard was from a very drunk receptionist who wanted to tell me all about how Rigman used to stare down her shirt and make inappropriate comments. Someone might quit over that, but most people wouldn't kill over it." He straightened up completely and met my gaze. "I know you don't want to hear it, but I think Strobel's on the right track with Eve Tudor. I overheard a lot of people talking about how they didn't blame her for killing him."

I'd been hoping Dan hadn't heard the same whisperings I had. Eve had already been tried in the court of public opinion even though she hadn't been arrested yet. "She wants to find the truth as much as I do."

His eyes softened at the edges in a way that made him look tired beyond physical exhaustion. "Unfortunately, *helping* with an investigation is common for guilty people. They use it as a way to try to keep track of the investigation and direct it away from themselves. It's why I suspected you when I found out you were poking around into Grandpa's death."

Jarrod had said the same thing about people who tried to insert themselves into an investigation. Which could explain why I wanted to deny it. I hated to think that Jarrod had been right about anything.

If Dan were right, if that was Eve's true motivation, then her friendship with me was also a lie. As selfish as it might be, I'd rather accept that she killed someone than that she'd been playing me. Coming back from that...I wasn't sure I could come back from that. It'd been so hard to find friends.

My first friend since I ran away from Jarrod, Nicole Fitzhenry-Dawes-Cavanaugh, was miles away and I couldn't contact her often for fear that I'd accidentally make her a target for Jarrod. Dan had been my second friend, and he'd convinced me I was safer with friends than without them.

I didn't know how to reconcile that with the risk that people would pretend to be my friends to serve their our purposes. I'd proven I wasn't a good enough judge of character to figure out when someone was genuine and when they weren't.

So perhaps I was lying to myself about Eve. Perhaps I only wanted her to be innocent and wanted her to be my friend because I didn't have very many of those.

Regardless it gave me even more motivation to prove her innocent. If she were innocent, our new friendship was a real one. "I think there's an option other than Eve. Do you know if Detective Strobel has looked into the caterer who was supposed to be working the barbecue?"

I explained my theory to him based on what I knew about the food industry.

Dan rubbed a hand around the back of his neck, something he tended to do when he was facing a dilemma that he didn't know how to solve. "Strobel's a bit territorial about his cases, and

I've already nosed in once. I can try to casually drop the caterer's name and see what he says. Who was supposed to be catering the event?"

I texted Eve, and she replied almost immediately. "Kaylani Mitchell. Her business is Casa Bella Catering." I turned my phone around so Dan could see my screen. "She even sent me the phone number."

Dan's look said *And you're saying she's not overeager about the investigation?* But he didn't actually speak the words, so I couldn't argue with him.

DAN CALLED ME THE NEXT DAY AS I WAS OUTSIDE MY TRUCK, setting up at my usual lunch location. I checked the message he left as soon as I got back inside.

"Strobel wasn't happy that a potential source keeps sharing information with me rather than going to him," Dan's message said. "He wants a name. I told him my source prefers to remain anonymous. He seemed to think I was lying to him because I thought he wasn't competent. Unless we have concrete evidence in the future, we won't be able to pass leads along to him anymore. He's unlikely to even consider them without something solid, and he's threatened to report me for interfering in investigations that I'm not assigned to."

That was the last thing I wanted to have happen. Dan

shouldn't face a reprimand because I insisted we try to solve the case ourselves.

I called him back.

"I'm sorry for causing trouble," I said in lieu of a hello. "I guess I thought he'd be more interested in solving the case than in protecting his pride."

Dan sighed. "I think he will be in time."

I leaned a shoulder against my truck. "So we have no way of knowing if he's already looked into the caterer?"

"Not exactly. During his rant, he did let slip that Kaylani Mitchell has an alibi for time of death. She couldn't have done it. I think we're out of options. We'll have to leave it up to Strobel from here on out."

I stuffed my disappointment down, but it wouldn't stay there.

Not only was Kaylani Mitchell not a viable person of inter-est, but it suddenly felt like the only two people who didn't have an alibi for Anthony Rigman's murder were Eve and me. With Strobel now on the warpath and no other suspects, that didn't bode well for either of us.

---

13

*T*he first big drops of rain pinged off the metal of my truck, sounding like a marriage between wind chimes and a kettle drum, and cutting off any further business for the day.

For once, it didn't stress me out. I'd pick up the second half of my payment from Rigman & Associates soon. I had a birthday party to supply cupcakes with tomorrow. In fact, stopping early today would give me the time I needed to prep for tomorrow without feeling rushed.

I drove to one of my favorite out-of-the-way spaces. The rain picked up, turning from a few drops to a downpour. With the noise of the rain on the metal, I wouldn't be able to hear anyone approaching. Even though Dan had thrown Jarrod off my trail when he'd figured out I was in Lakeshore a few months ago, I still didn't want to be blind.

I slipped out into the rain and popped open the front flap. The rain was coming from the other direction, so opening it allowed me to see out and cut down on the heat inside without getting everything wet.

Since I couldn't hear anything but the rain anyway, I pulled out my phone and cued up some music. It'd been so long since I'd allowed myself music while I worked. Listening to it, I could almost forget that I was still a suspect in a murder and still on the run from a man who wanted to hurt me.

I could be a teenager again. Before my dad died and everything else went wrong. The rain always made me think of him. Florida got so hot in the summer that we rarely went outside. Whenever it would rain, we'd run out and spin around, arms wide in our own crazy version of a rain dance.

When Jarrod and I were first married, I used to beg him to go out and dance with me in the rain. He told me to grow up. I didn't have the courage to defy the look he gave me when he said it.

Years had passed since I'd enjoyed the rain. I wasn't with Jarrod anymore. He controlled so much of my life simply by virtue of the fact that I had to be afraid of him finding me, but he couldn't control this anymore. If I didn't know when he might find me, I might as well enjoy every moment and make it all count.

I cranked up the volume on my phone as loud as it would go, threw open the door to my truck, and stepped out into the rain.

Just like when I was a kid, I stuck out my arms and spun around, slowly at first, then faster and faster.

A blur moved at the edge of my vision. I tripped and caught myself on the bumper, my heart beat louder in my ears than the rain on the roof of my truck. I backed up a step and wiped the rain out of my eyes.

Dan stood ten feet away, the collar of his jacket popped up against the rain.

I couldn't read the expression on his face. Heat burned up my neck. As if I didn't seem weird enough to him already, he had to catch me at this.

I expected him to ask what I was doing. Or to laugh at me.

Instead, he stuck out his hand. "May I have the rest of this dance?" he asked, his voice raised over the noise of the rain.

Before I could overthink it, I slid my hand into his. His palm was warm compared to the rain raising goosebumps on my skin.

He spun me out, then back in, following the beat of the song. We broke apart and danced alone, then came back together to spin again. At first, all I could think about was how silly I must look, but Dan didn't seem to care. By the end of the song, we were both laughing, and I could barely catch my breath.

I motioned him inside my truck and turned the music off. We stood in the small space, dripping all over my floor.

I tossed him a hand towel. It was the best I had to offer unless I wanted to open my small storage space to get him one of the two full-sized towels I owned. I couldn't do that without him catching sight of the sleeping bag and pillow I also stored in there.

He dried off his face and ruffled his hair. It stood up slightly when he was done, giving me a glimpse of what he must have looked like in his early twenties. He looked even more attractive than he did in his suit or his pink How Sweet It Is t-shirt.

I was suddenly aware my clothes were sticking to me in a way that was uncomfortable—and not because of the dampness. My shirt clung to my less-than-perfect body. At least I hadn't been wearing a white shirt like Helen Hunt's character in that scene in *As Good As It Gets*.

I pulled my shirt away from my skin slightly, trying not to make it obvious.

"Looks like Claire and I were worried about nothing," Dan said. His tone was light, but it felt a bit forced.

My throat clamped tight. "Is Detective Strobel coming to arrest me?"

For the briefest second Dan looked like he was going to ask me if there was a reason Strobel should arrest me. It passed quickly enough that I recognized it for what it was—his cop's tendency to be suspicious. As soon as his logical brain took back over, whatever instinctive reaction he'd seemed to have vanished.

"Nothing to do with the case." Dan glanced down to the growing puddle at his feet and the already damp towel in his hand as if realizing there wasn't much point in trying to dry himself off further. He looked as uncertain as I'd ever seen him. "Claire tried to call you to ask if you wanted her to keep that second freezer in case you needed it to freeze cupcakes again in the future. When all her calls went to voicemail, she called me. I thought…"

The tightness in his voice wrapped around my chest. He'd thought Jarrod found me. "My ringer must have gotten turned off accidentally. I'll text Claire right away."

Dan nodded and cleared his throat. I sent Claire a quick message telling her I was alright and that I'd call her in a few minutes. Then I checked my ringer. At some point, I'd accidentally flipped the button that silenced my phone. I had almost ten missed calls from Claire and Dan. They'd been trying to reach me for hours.

I hit send on the text. Dan's concern might not be unwarranted if he'd been able to locate me. I'd never told him about this spot. If he could spot me, so could Jarrod if he decided to look here again. "How did you find me?"

Dan glanced away, avoiding my gaze. "I called in a favor and had a friend of mine in the department ping your cell phone. Once he narrowed down the location for me, I drove around until I spotted your truck."

A shiver ran over my spine, but I couldn't figure out if it was because locating me that way was possible or because I finally had someone who cared enough about what happened to me to call in favors. The fact that Fear wasn't screaming in my brain made me think it was the latter.

"Thank you," my words came out a little more strangled than I'd intended.

Dan nodded again, and his undercover cop mask slid back on his face. He rubbed his hand around the back of his neck as if he were still trying to shake off the fear that must have dogged his steps the whole way here. "Why do you need to freeze cupcakes anyway?"

At least he hadn't asked me why I needed to use Claire's freezer rather than using one in my own place. Hopefully Claire had told him that my apartment was too small for a full-sized freezer, and I wouldn't have to outright lie to Dan as well.

"So they stay fresh. If I have to prepare ahead for a bigger event." I reached into my fridge and pulled out a couple of cupcakes that I'd baked a few days ago and hadn't managed to sell as day-olds. Even storing them in the fridge, they'd started to dry out. I ate any leftovers anyway rather than letting them go to waste, but most people wouldn't pay for something this shriveled. I handed him one of the older cupcakes. "This is what happens otherwise."

Dan bit into the cupcake. "It is a little dry." He frowned. "Why do the cupcakes you can buy in the store stay good for weeks?"

I considered quibbling that the cupcakes you could buy individually packaged in the store were never good. Then I remembered that Dan had come to me rather than going to a grocery store to buy cupcakes when Janie needed them for school. He'd also come out in the rain to find me when he thought I might be in trouble. I didn't need to get touchy over nothing. He knew my cupcakes were better than the prepackaged ones at the store. He wasn't comparing quality. He was simply asking why those ones lasted three or four times longer than mine.

"Preservatives," I said, speaking extra loudly so he could hear me over the pounding of the rain.

I bit into my own aged cupcake. It stuck in my throat.

Preservatives.

Could that be why everyone with a motive to murder Anthony Rigman had an alibi during the time-of-death window?

Dan had paused with the rest of his cupcake halfway to his mouth. "You look like you're trying not to choke. They're not that bad. Promise."

I shook my head. "It's not that. Could Anthony Rigman have been given something that would make it look like he'd been dead less time than he had?"

Dan's eyes narrowed as if he were concentrating on something I couldn't see. "Arsenic could have done it, but that's part of the regular toxicology panel. If he'd been poisoned with arsenic, then the medical examiner would have already adjusted the suspected time of death. Any other poisons that might act as a preservative are ones I haven't encountered."

The rain had stopped outside. I no longer felt like I had to shout to be heard, but the ringing sound seemed to linger in my ears. "Could you ask the medical examiner?"

He smoothed back his hair, but it popped upright again, already half dry. "Technically, no. It's not my case. Strobel would be the one to ask for an additional work-up, and he won't do it if I come to him with a vague hunch again. There's no way I can go to the medical examiner without it getting back to him."

Dan had said that before. We had to have something concrete before he could take it to Strobel. Dan had worn out his professional courtesy.

If we couldn't ask the medical examiner to test for something specific, we needed to at least know if there were other options that could have preserved the body and thrown off the time of death. We also needed to know whether it would change the window by weeks, days, or only a few hours. A few hours wouldn't matter, but a few days definitely would.

It'd also explain why I hadn't seen or heard anything while I was parked beside the beach making cupcakes for the sandcastle competition. And why there hadn't been any footprints or drag marks. Anthony would have been killed and buried long before I showed up. Long before the people in charge of the competition had smoothed the sand.

I knew of someone who might be able to help us, but contacting her directly could put her at risk. Jarrod would use her to get to me if he even suspected she knew where I was or how to contact me. Knowing her condition, I wanted to do that even less now than I had before.

"I know someone who might be able to help." I held out a hand. "May I borrow your phone?"

Dan pulled it from his pocket. It was a little moist but not soaked. "Is your phone dead?"

I shook my head. "It's safer this way."

Confusion flashed over his face, but it vanished in the time it took for him to extend the phone to me. He'd rushed to find me because he thought Jarrod might have already found me. He was the one person who might understand why I went to such lengths to protect people who knew I wasn't actually Isabel Addington.

I dialed the number.

"Nicole Cavanaugh...err...Fitzhenry-Dawes...It's Nicole."

The voice on the other end of the line held a touch of self-frustration. I smiled despite my reason for calling. The way she answered was very Nicole-like. Her married name was Cavanaugh, but she still practiced law under her maiden name. "It's me."

"Isabel? Are you okay?"

The fact that she felt the need to ask that but didn't ask where I was spoke volumes. "I'm okay. I'm helping a friend, but I need to ask Mark a question."

"He's right here. Let me put him on speaker."

She didn't even hesitate. Tears pressed at the back of my

eyes. Nicole had been my first friend when I hadn't even realized how much I needed one. I missed her.

There was a bit of a rustling noise.

"You have us both now," Mark Cavanaugh's voice said. It sounded like he was speaking from a distance, but I could still hear him clearly.

I tapped the speaker phone icon on Dan's phone as well, so he could listen in. "I'm here with Detective Dan Holmes of the Lakeshore police. We're wondering if there's a poison that could make a dead body look fresher than it actually is."

"Arsenic's the most common one," Mark said, "but if you're asking, that must not have shown up in the tox screen. There's also antimony."

I typed it into the search bar on my phone. The websites that came up showed what looked like a gray rock. I wasn't sure what form that rock had to be turned into to poison someone, but the site I'd pulled up first said that factory workers made up the majority of accidental antimony poisoning cases.

"It's colorless, odorless, and tasteless, so it's easy for someone who comes in contact with it to experience even accidental poisoning," Mark was saying, almost like he'd been standing beside me and saw what I was reading. "But your ME should have been able to tell you that, Detective."

Dan shifted beside me. "It's not exactly my case."

I thought I heard a sound in the background like Nicole had snort-laughed.

"Okay." Mark drew the word out as if he wasn't sure what Nicole had gotten him into this time, but he'd learned to go with it. "Well, if your victim was poisoned with antimony, you won't be able to get a clear TOD from the body. You'll need to use contextual clues instead. The body could be weeks old but look days old."

If that were the case with Anthony Rigman, it opened up the suspect pool again.

Dan leaned close. "The last day anyone saw Rigman alive was the day after the argument you broke up between him and Eve," he whispered. "He was supposed to leave for a conference the next morning. He didn't show up. Strobel discounted that because the body seemed to be fresh, and Rigman had a history of canceling plans at the last minute. But if he has antimony in his system, that means he could have been killed any time after he left work the day of the argument."

Our suspect pool would be wide open again. I still didn't think Harper did it. Her angry message sounded like she had no idea he was dead, and that would have likely been after he'd been killed.

The caterer, Kaylani Mitchell, though, might have.

Muffled voices carried through Mark and Nicole's end of the line. It sounded like Nicole had said something close to *Is there any way we can help?*

"You said you're in Lakeshore?" Mark asked.

Dan took the phone from me to hold it closer to his mouth. "That's right."

"I know your ME. He and I have consulted together a few times on difficult cases. I'll give him a call and suggest he run an extra test for antimony. I'll also ask him to tell the detective in charge that he had a hunch. That way the investigation won't be looking in the wrong places and also won't be held up by someone's toes being stepped on."

The tone of Mark's voice said he didn't have a lot of patience for grandstanding and being worried about who'd get the credit when it came to solving a crime. No wonder he and Nicole made such a great team.

"Thank you," Dan and I said at the same time.

We might not be a couple like Mark and Nicole were, but we seemed to make a pretty good team.

14

We'd just finished Sunday night dinner, and I was helping Dan wash and dry the dishes while Claire got Janie ready for bed.

Dan's cell phone pinged with a text, and he dried his hands on a dish cloth. He glanced at the screen. "It's from Mark Cavanaugh. He says he didn't know if we'd have a way to find out, and he wanted us to know that our hunch was right. Anthony Rigman died of antimony poisoning."

Relief rushed through me. That made all the difference. Or it could make all the difference. The suspects who'd had concrete alibis were now possibilities again. Eve and I weren't the only ones.

"Mark also wanted us to know that antimony poisoning doesn't mean Rigman couldn't have died when the medical examiner originally thought. It just means the window of death is larger."

Much larger. A whole week larger. Anthony Rigman could have been killed at any point during the week between the argument I'd broken up and the sandcastle competition. Detective Strobel would probably still think Eve and I were the most likely suspects unfortunately. Just because he could have been killed at some other time didn't mean he was.

But I was confident now that he had been. I barely sleep most nights listening for footsteps outside my truck. There's no way I could have been so tired or distracted that I wouldn't have heard someone burying a body right in front of me. "It seems like the day after he argued on the street with Eve makes the most sense. Otherwise, someone would have seen him or heard from him during that time. He'd have gone to work."

"He didn't have many messages on his answering machine."

"True. But we don't know if that's because most people called his cell phone rather than his house phone or if it's because he was playing them."

Dan moved next to me and leaned against the counter, so we were both facing out in the same direction. "Would I be right in guessing you're planning to continue investigating now that a lot of the people of interest are back on the table?"

I nodded, turned back to the sink, washed the final plate, and handed it to him.

Dan accepted the plate from me. "If I know Strobel, he'll be re-interviewing everyone who knew Rigman to see if he can figure out the last time someone spoke to him. Now that he has a bigger gap for a possible time of death, he'll want to narrow it down."

I stripped off the yellow rubber gloves. I couldn't even take myself seriously while wearing them. "I'd like to start with the caterer."

He shifted beside me, and I looked up to meet his gaze. Standing side by side this way, we were close enough that I could smell the peppermint he'd popped into his mouth after dinner. He was looking down at me.

My brain felt like it suddenly ground to a halt, and it took me a minute to realize I hadn't asked if he was still onboard. "Assuming you're still willing to help me. We do work well together, and you said you wanted to keep me out of trouble."

Claire's footsteps approached from behind. I stepped back. My cheeks suddenly felt hot. Which was ridiculous. We hadn't been doing anything other than talking.

Claire's eyes narrowed slightly and the look she gave said *am I interrupting something?*

"We're into the case too deep to stop now." Dan's voice was scratchier than usual. "The caterer it is."

Claire planted her hands on her hips. "How do you expect to do that? Neither of you are officially investigating this case, and you told me Detective Strobel already wanted to have a reprimand placed in your file."

I flinched. Dan had downplayed it for me when he'd told me how Detective Strobel reacted. I'd gotten him in trouble at work.

My shoulders hunched forward. I wanted to collapse in on myself and slink from the room, but Claire stood between me and the door. The expression on her face said her question hadn't been hypothetical.

I frowned. She wasn't trying to stop us then? She was just trying to make sure we had a plan that wouldn't end up with one of us in trouble?

Dan took my hand, linking his fingers with mine, and held it up. "Don't you recognize my fiancé? We need to interview caterers for our wedding. No one can have a problem with that."

My brain stopped working altogether. His hand was warm and firm, but it felt different with our fingers intertwined than it had that first time he'd shaken my hand. It was such an intimate gesture, palm to palm.

The rational side of me knew this was a great front for a caterer, and that Dan had plenty of experience with undercover roles. Another side of me couldn't help remembering the time we'd both been investigating his grandfather's murder, and there was an onion ring misunderstanding. Dan made a joke about getting engaged before we'd even had a first date.

It'd saddened me then, but it hadn't turned me into a mind-numbed jellyfish.

"Are you and Isabel getting married?" Janie's tiny voice said from the doorway.

I yanked my hand from Dan's as if he'd given me a shock. Janie stood just inside the kitchen in her Disney princess pajamas, a stuffed bunny clutched in her arms.

"Isabel and I were just playing make-believe." Dan scooped her off the ground and carried her out of the room. "You must be ready for your story?"

"It'd be okay if it were for real." Janie's voice was barely audible and getting softer. "Then Isabel could live here all the time."

My eyes felt like they were full of grit. I blinked hard. There was no way to explain to a five-year-old that her wish could never be. All the things I'd have to explain to her like abuse and divorce to make her understand were things she shouldn't know about for years yet.

Besides, Dan was my friend. I wasn't even trying for anything more. I wasn't ready for anything more even if I'd been free to date someone.

And a man like Dan could have pretty much any woman he wanted. He wouldn't want a mess like me. Even someone with a good heart had to have his limits for how much baggage he could overlook. I'd be an idiot to even let myself daydream. My heart had enough stab wounds in it. I didn't need to self-inflict any more.

I looked away from the door, and my gaze snagged on

Claire's. She'd been watching me.

"She's lost a lot already," Claire said. "Janie I mean."

As if I could have thought she meant anyone else.

She didn't need to warn me away from Dan. I knew better than she did that nothing would ever happen there.

So all I could do in response was nod.

15

I pulled the seatbelt of Dan's car slightly away from my chest. It'd started to feel like it was crushing the air out of my lungs. "I'm not sure this is a good idea after all."

The closer we got to the catering company, the harder it was for me to get what Claire and Dan had both said about Detective Strobel out of my head. I had to continue investigating, for my sake and for Eve's. Dan didn't. He didn't need to put his career at stake. He had a little girl to support. And if he got fired, would he even be able to get another job in his field? Not to mention a job in another city would mean leaving his family behind. Leaving Claire behind. She'd never forgive me.

I gulped in a large breath and nearly choked on it. "You could drop me off, and I could tell the caterer that my fiancé couldn't make it. I'm sure that happens a lot. Some men aren't even interested in wedding details, only the honeymoon."

Shoot. That sounded bad. Now he'd think I was saying that all men only cared about sex.

"Do I need to get you a bag? You look like you're about to hyperventilate." Dan's voice had taken on that tone I'd come to recognize as his first responder voice. It was the voice that said *I got this* and *everything's going to be okay*. "If you're worried I'll blow your cover, I'm the one with the experience, remember?"

He gave me that smile that made me feel like he really could make anything happen. I was willing to risk a lot more than I had been half a year ago in order to see justice done, but his and Janie and Claire's welfare weren't one of those things.

His smile faded. He pulled the car over in front of Casa Bella Catering. "Okay, what's on your mind? If we go in like this, the caterer will think we're fighting."

That dragged a little smile from me. If we'd actually been fighting, it was more likely no one would have been able to tell when they saw me. In that kind of situation, I was great at hiding the truth. Case in point was that Dan hadn't figured out I was living in my truck.

"I don't want to risk you getting fired for helping me." Claire's words last night zinged back into my mind in a different context. "Janie's lost too much already."

"Good." He didn't wink, but I heard one in this voice. "I'd hate to think you didn't want to even try imagining what it'd be like to be engaged to me." His expression sobered. "When I worked undercover, I saw too many situations that looked like they should be safe turn bad. Having something happen to you when I could have prevented it would be worse for Janie than anything that could happen with my job." His smile peeked out again. "Besides, Strobel's on shaky ground if he does complain. I'm not impeding his investigation in any way, and I'm not neglecting my own cases. I'm doing all of this on personal time, and if anything, I've helped him."

I'd lived with a law enforcement officer before. I knew that investigating cases on personal time wasn't exactly kosher. As long as Dan didn't use his influence as a police officer though, it wasn't exactly forbidden either. He couldn't be dismissed for talking to people any more than I could be charged with a crime for talking to people—as long as nothing we did hurt the official case.

He unbuckled his seatbelt, went around the car, and opened my door for me. "Come on, darling. We don't want to be late for our appointment."

I took the hand he offered and tried to ignore the way the warmth of it seemed to tingle up my arm. "Darling?"

"Too black-and-white movie?"

I nodded.

"Honey?"

It sounded so natural coming out of his mouth that, hearing it, I could almost forget we weren't really a couple, nor were we ever likely to be one. "Honey works."

He linked his fingers with mine the way he had the night

before. His hands were bigger than mine, but not so big that the hold would be uncomfortable, even over time. Instead, it felt secure.

That feeling was almost worse than if it'd felt threatening. At least if it'd felt threatening, I wouldn't have wanted to leave my hand in his.

He gave my hand two quick squeezes as if to say *we can do this* and pushed open the door.

The young woman behind the counter was in her twenties and leaned toward plump. Her hair was pulled up into an updo, revealing a single purple stripe, and tattoos covered all the bare skin on her arms.

She grinned at us and came out from behind the counter. "You must be Dan and Isabel. I'm Tina, and I'll be walking you through our catering options."

She shook Dan's hand first, then mine. She held onto my hand a moment extra. "You look really familiar. Have we met before?"

I had the sense that this wasn't the first time I'd seen her either. Likely we'd both been at an event at some point. If I didn't confess to that, and she figured it out, she might think we were lying about why we were here. Which, of course, we were, but she'd likely assume it was because we were trying to do a little bakery espionage rather than that we were investigating a murder.

"I run How Sweet It Is, a cupcake truck." I put the smile on my face that I used to give to Jarrod whenever he gave me an expensive present that showed how little he actually knew me. It'd fooled him every time. "One thing I know from what I do for work is that you never want to cater your own event."

She pursed her lips in a way that said *ain't that the truth*. "Kaylani catered my wedding last summer, and it was bad enough having my boss and co-workers serving. I kept feeling like I should pitch in." She motioned to one of the tables in the corner of the shop. "Why don't you two take a seat over there, and I'll be right back with a list of what we can do and our wedding packages."

That sounded like she was going to be the one sitting down with us. She hadn't said *take a seat while I get Kaylani*.

We sat, and I leaned my head closer to Dan's so Tina wouldn't overhear. "We might not get anything out of this if Kaylani isn't even here."

Dan's nose bumped my cheek as he turned to speak into my ear in return. The contact sent a weird shiver down into my stomach.

"Kaylani is the one I spoke to on the phone. She didn't say she wouldn't be the one meeting with us."

Tina came back toward us with a sheaf of papers tucked under her arm, a plate with goodies in one hand, and a glass of water in the other. She smiled again, and it was so natural that it made me think she was just a naturally smiley person rather than that she was wearing it as part of her uniform. "I hope you two don't mind sharing."

Dan leaned closer as if he might kiss my cheek for show. I stiffened, and he stopped before he reached me.

"Of course not," he said, with a cheeky grin.

Tina laid out all our options while Dan and I nibbled on the squares and tarts she'd brought us. Eating them felt wrong since we weren't actually considering hiring Casa Bella Catering, but it wasn't like she'd put them back in the display to sell now anyway. That'd be a health code violation.

Dan ate a few items on the tasting plate too, but he didn't touch the water. He didn't know if I would, in fact, mind sharing a glass with him, so he must have decided to leave it for me. My throat closed slightly. It was such a small, thoughtful gesture.

Once she finished, Dan looked over at me. That was my cue. We'd planned out our own version of good cop-bad cop.

I scooted closer and linked my arm with his, holding his hand once again. Tina wouldn't be able to see our hands under the table, but it was the only place I could really lay my palm other than on Dan's thigh, and I wasn't doing that. The warmth from his arm and hand already made me too aware of how close we sat.

I gave him a look that said *pretty please*. "This looks perfect for an outdoor wedding."

His expression carried the perfect balance of uncertainty and desire to please.

Watching him and knowing he'd worked undercover before his brother died and he adopted Janie, it was easy to see how good he must have been. He was good enough that he could have been an actor on screen or in an improv show.

"Ed did tell me…" He trailed off and shot a fake surreptitious glance at Tina. "We should probably go home and discuss it before we make a decision."

We couldn't be certain someone named Ed worked for Rigman & Associates, but with a company with multiple offices, it seemed like a safe bet. Besides, Rigman & Associates was too large for Tina to know everyone who worked there even if they had catered for them for years.

"If you have any questions, I'd be happy to answer them." Tina's tone carried the right amount of deference. She seemed to know better than to hard sell. There were a lot of bakeries and caterers in Lakeshore. Anyone who pushed too hard would likely lose the sale altogether.

Dan sighed and angled to face her. "I'll be honest with you. We were hoping to talk to Ms. Mitchell before making a decision. Is she here?"

Tina's body language stayed completely relaxed. If what Dan said insulted her at all, she didn't show it. "Not today, unfortunately. She sprained her ankle last night, and the doctor told her that if she wanted to be able to work this summer she needed to stay off of it for two weeks minimum. But I promise that I can handle whatever you need. I've worked with Kaylani since she opened almost ten years ago."

At least we hadn't gotten a new hire. Perhaps this visit wouldn't be a waste after all. Tina should know why they'd given up the catering job with Rigman & Associates.

Dan gave me that look that couples exchange when they're checking in with each other. It meant something completely different to me than Tina would assume. I nodded.

Dan leaned forward slightly as if about to make a confession. "Look. A buddy of mine works for an insurance company that's hired you guys in the past. Izzy loves your food and wants to work with you, but he warned me that you left them in the lurch at the last minute. I was hoping to talk to Ms. Mitchell, so she could clear it up before we committed."

Something in the way Dan held himself and the way he'd changed the cadence of his speech from how he normally sounded made me think he was playing the role of a man who worked with his hands—a construction worker or a mechanic maybe. I couldn't have pinpointed what it was, only that I'd have guessed one of those as his profession if I'd been asked. It made him seem down to earth, while at the same time seeming like someone who wasn't going to tolerate her sidestepping his concerns. It made him seem like he couldn't possibly be lying.

Tina brought in a breath slowly and let it out. "Rigman and Associates, right?"

Dan nodded.

"That was a personal matter that wouldn't ever happen again?"

A lot of what Anthony Rigman did to other people could be called a *personal matter*. He'd been controlling and verbally abusive with Eve. He'd made the work environment so toxic for Harper that she felt her only option was to quit, and then out of spite he'd blocked her from getting another position.

I could only imagine what *personal matter* could have pushed a caterer to quit a long-standing client. My mind immediately jumped to him raping her, and I prayed that wasn't what had happened.

I worked a concerned expression onto my face. My training ground had been different from Dan's, but I was no amateur in play acting. "I'm in the same field. That could be considered personal reasons for cancelling on us too. I don't know if we can take that risk."

I cast a longing look toward their display cases as if I hated to walk away from their food. Though, to be honest, I couldn't remember what any of it tasted like. Either it hadn't been memorable or I was too distracted, the way you could eat a whole bag of potato chips in front of the TV if you weren't paying attention.

Tina tugged on her earlobe. Her gaze shifted from me to the papers she'd brought over, then on to the plate where a single square sat. I could also see her trying to decide whether securing us as clients would be worth sharing the truth about what had happened.

She gave her earlobe one final tug. "I'd like it if you kept this to yourself. I don't know if you can get sued for libel or slander for a dead person or whatever, but I don't want to risk it."

"Of course," Dan said without any hesitation.

Technically, we weren't going to go advertising what she'd said. Depending on what we learned, though, she might be focusing the light of a criminal investigation on her boss.

I cleared all that from my mind so it wouldn't show on my face. Sometimes not thinking about what you were really feeling and thinking was the only way to keep up an act.

Tina straightened the papers and nudged them a bit in my direction, almost as if she were subconsciously still hoping she wouldn't have to tell us what had happened.

"Kaylani was married to one of the owners of Rigman and Associates at the same time that he and his partner were launching their company. Kay basically supported him while he worked for free to get the company off the ground. Then as soon as he started getting successful, he left her."

Ouch. That was a great motive for murder if it'd happened recently, but Rigman & Associates had been around for years. Other than the national brands, they were the biggest insurance company in the area with three offices. Waiting this long to take her revenge didn't make sense.

Neither did the fact that she was catering for her ex-husband who'd treated her so badly. My confusion and disgust must have shown on my face. Tina nodded.

"I know, right? Thankfully Kay's brother was a divorce attorney. Unless Kay's ex wanted to lose half of his half of the business, he had to agree to supporting her in some way while she launched her own business. Part of that was that Rigman and Associates would have to exclusively use her business for catering for as long as she wanted."

Financially that would have been beneficial. Most new businesses failed within the first year. Having a built-in major client, with all the ancillary business that would generate from their employees experiencing her food, would have almost guaranteed her business took off.

"So she decided she no longer needed their business?" I asked.

Tina shook her head. "Not exactly. Anthony, her ex, did the whole letter of the law but not the spirit thing. Every time we had to work for him, he made it a miserable experience. Kay couldn't take it anymore." Tina rolled her eyes. "Too bad we didn't know someone was going to kill him. With him gone, we would have gladly kept the contract with Rigman and Associates."

A heavy weight settled on my shoulders. That was the opposite of what I wanted to hear. No one would believe Kaylani Mitchell would have cancelled her contract with Rigman & Associates and then killed Anthony. It didn't benefit her. If she'd killed him, she would have kept the contract, knowing that her working experience was about to greatly improve with him gone.

Something could have happened after she quit the contract to make her snap, but it'd be a hard sell to the district attorney, let alone to a jury.

Dan got to his feet. "Thanks for sharing that. Izzy and I will talk it over, but that helped a lot."

"Oh." A frown slid across Tina's face, but she quickly replaced it with a smile. "Yes. You know how to reach me. I wouldn't wait long, though. Summer is the busiest season for weddings, and we book a year in advance so if you want us to cater for next summer, now's the time."

I gave the regular assurances that we'd contact her as soon as we could, slid my arm through Dan's as if that were the most natural thing in the world, and let him lead me out the door.

I didn't say anything until he'd helped me back into the car and climbed into the driver's seat himself.

Once he pulled away from the curb, I drooped my head back against the head rest. "Detective Strobel won't consider her, will he." It was more of a statement than a question. I knew the answer, but I couldn't give up hope until I heard Dan confirm my suspicions.

"She doesn't seem like a likely enough suspect. Especially not compared to Eve."

"You keep saying that, but you can't give me any proof that I shouldn't trust her."

The words were out before I could stop them. My body instinctively shrank away from him, close to the door. My heartrate jumped like I was out after dark alone and caught motion in my peripheral vision.

Dan's gaze stayed on the road. "You know I can't. There's only so far I can push the lines."

He sounded factual, not angry. Not even annoyed.

The pounding of my blood in my head eased. Dan wasn't the kind of man who'd get angry with me because I lost my patience or defended my friend. Intellectually I'd known that, but something inside me gave a little seeing it again.

I forced my body to relax. "I know," I said softly. "And I wouldn't want you to."

His gaze slid to me and away again. "I've seen the evidence. It speaks to a pattern. If it were my case, I would suspect her too."

In other words, he'd been helping me investigate this case not because he believed Eve was innocent the way I did. He'd been helping me because it was important to me and because he wanted to be sure I was safe.

I didn't know how to feel about that.

16

*S*tanding in the Rigman & Associates lobby, waiting for the receptionist to retrieve my check, I couldn't get Dan's words out of my head.

If it were my case, I would suspect her too.

I didn't trust a lot of people, but I did trust Dan. Not just as a human being. I trusted his investigative skills and instincts. Beyond that, he was objective about this case. His suspicions about Eve weren't because he wanted a quick solve to the case—though detectives always wanted to solve cases as quickly as possible.

Dan had seemed genuinely concerned when he'd asked me to be careful about Eve. He said there was evidence.

The receptionist returned and passed me my check. "I missed the barbecue, but I heard the food was amazing. I hope you'll be doing our Christmas party too."

I hadn't thought about that. If the majority of employees had enjoyed my food, maybe they would hire me again for Christmas and then for next year's annual barbecue. Eve might have just handed me a long-term business relationship. The only other situation I had that fit was the Friday cupcake tray I delivered to a business that had concerns about nuts. If I could get a few more repeat customers who were businesses, I wouldn't feel so pressured about money and getting the best spots for the lunchtime rush.

Had I thanked her? I didn't think I had. I'd been so hesitant about it at first because I wasn't sure why the other caterer quit, and then I'd been looking at it from the perspective of finding other suspects for Anthony's murder. I should thank her. At least part of her reasons for getting me the job had been to help me.

The receptionist's smile faded slightly, and her eyebrows arched up in a question. How long had I been standing there, staring into space?

"Eve Tudor is a friend of mine. I thought I'd pop in and say hi. Can you point me in the direction of her office?"

"Sure thing."

She must have assumed my mental lapse was me deciding whether to bother Eve at work. She led me past the offices where agents were speaking with potential customers. Their doors were glass, but shut for confidentiality.

I knew we'd reached the non-insurance agent staff when the glass doors turned to solid doors.

The receptionist knocked on the doorframe beside an open door. "You have a visitor."

"Ooo, you know I love guests." Eve's voice was bubbly. "Any excuse to take a break."

The receptionist motioned me in. "Don't let her silliness fool you. She's one of the hardest working people here."

I gave her an I'm-in-on-the-secret smile and headed in.

Eve came forward with her arms held in a way that made me think she planned to hug me. I stiffened before I could stop myself. It wasn't that I had a problem being touched per se. Janie hugged me all the time, and I'd gotten used to being touched by Dan. If I were being honest, before Dan took me in as a quasi-family member, I'd missed being touched.

I just needed to be prepared for it, so I could remind my body that normal touch didn't hurt.

Eve stopped partway to me as if she'd spotted my hesitancy. "Is everything okay?"

Something in her voice made me think that she was worried I'd learned something negative about Anthony's murder investigation. As if she were scared of what I might have found.

If she were innocent, would she be frightened of what I might have uncovered?

I was innocent, and I was frightened. I was frightened of what Detective Strobel might uncover about who I was. I was also frightened because I actually had something to hide.

So she could be frightened that she'd go to prison for something she didn't do if enough evidence piled up against her. Or she could be frightened because she had done it, and she was worried I'd uncovered something that would help prove her guilt. I had no way of knowing which.

"I came to pick up the rest of my payment."

I stupidly held up my check as if she would need proof that's why I came. That was definitely my own guilt showing through. Shouldn't I believe her? Shouldn't her word have been enough for me when she said she hadn't killed Anthony? It felt like it should if we were truly friends. But that was the rub. If she were guilty, we weren't really friends at all.

But if she was innocent, and we were friends, I didn't want her to think I was ungrateful for the opportunity she'd given me. "And I wanted to thank you for getting me the job in the first place."

Eve's entire face seemed to lift, from the corners of her lips to her eyebrows. "We should be thanking you for taking the job. No way were we going to find food that good anywhere else."

The compliment should have sent a warm tingle over my skin. Instead, I somehow felt like I was about to kick a puppy.

That said, if I was going to keep defending her to Dan, and if I was going to keep asking him to help me dig into this case at the risk of a reprimand from his superior officer, I needed to first be sure she'd told me the truth.

I peeked back out into the hallway. For the moment, no one was nearby. "I did find out a couple of things about the case."

Eve practically bounced on her toes. "A new suspect." She lowered down and stilled for a minute. "I know I shouldn't hope one of my co-workers killed Anthony, but it's better than me going to prison for something I didn't do."

There's your opening, Isabel, I prodded myself. *You have to be brave and take it or you're always going to wonder.*

Fear was silent in my head for a change. He must agree with my more rational side for once. To be Eve's friend going forward, I had to feel safe around her.

"Not exactly." My mouth felt like I'd eaten sand. "You're the main suspect because of some evidence they have against you. I don't know details, but I heard Anthony's death fits into a pattern."

Eve's face went white, and then two spots of red flared in her cheeks. "Are you kidding me?"

Her voice did a funny high-pitched squeak on the *me*. Her hands fluttered up like she was going to cover her mouth, then down again. Finally, she clasped them tight in front of her, her fingers a tangled mess.

"That was...that shouldn't even..." She stopped as if she didn't know how to finish any of what she'd started.

Her response could indicate guilt or it could indicate that she was afraid something innocent would be used against her. I didn't know her well enough to know which.

And I was too far in to let it drop. I wouldn't be able to think about anything else every time I saw her or talked to her.

"What are they talking about?" I kept my voice low and non-threatening.

The look she shot me felt like a slap.

"Knock knock." A man's voice said from the doorway. "Everything alright in here? I thought someone sounded upset, and you know we have a No Tolerance policy."

I turned around. Mr. Green stood in the doorway, his face just as red and glossy with sweat as when I'd met him at the barbecue, despite the extra-cold air conditioning in the building.

His words carried a chuckle under them. I couldn't tell if he was serious or not. The building did have signs everywhere that said abusive language or threats to the staff wouldn't be tolerated. Which, if you thought about it, was a bit ironic considering how Anthony Rigman had treated people.

Eve pasted on a smile that looked more plastic than the bracelet on her wrist. "Isabel and I were just talking about maybe switching her insurance for her truck over to Rigman and Associates. I couldn't believe how much she's been paying for insurance. Isabel practically lives in there, so she thought it was fair, but I think we can do better. I'm going to refer her to one of our agents to talk about it more."

Her look dared me to contradict her. Whatever made her a suspect, Mr. Green clearly didn't know about it. And she didn't want him to know. I couldn't exactly blame her. Everyone here already thought she was guilty, and that was without anything concrete like whatever it was that she was hiding.

Mr. Green motioned to the hallway. "I have a couple of minutes. I can go over everything with you now if you'd like Isabel. Given how you helped us out, we'll even give you the employee discount."

Not for the first time, I wondered how such a kind man ended up with a partner like Anthony. Then again, how had Eve ended up dating him? Maybe that was the nature of truly awful people. They preyed on those who were the least like them.

Though, Eve hadn't answered my question. She'd acted like she had no intention of answering it either before Mr. Green interrupted us. Whatever she was hiding had flustered her. She'd seemed like she was trying to hold in her temper.

Dan might be right. Detective Strobel might not be on a witch hunt after all where Eve was concerned.

I felt like someone had put me on a tilt-o-whirl. I couldn't stay in this building any longer, not even to keep up appearances.

I tucked my check into my pocket. "I have to get back to my truck, but I'll stop at the front desk and make an appointment for another day."

"Sure, sure," Mr. Green said. "You just make sure to ask for me. I'll give you the best deal possible."

Anthony Rigman had probably hated that about his partner. Anthony seemed to be the kind of man who did whatever it took to get ahead or get what he wanted. From everything I'd heard and seen, Mr. Green cared about the people behind the money.

It was too bad I wasn't in the market for insurance. Mr.

Green probably would give me a better deal than what I had. But right now, I needed to put some distance between Eve and me.

Mr. Green waved to me as I left. As soon as he turned away into his office, I walked past the front desk and didn't look back.

17

I rubbed at my eyes with the back of my arm and bit back a yawn. It'd been a long day, but a good one. With summer in full swing, Lakeshore's beaches were packed on the weekends. The weather this weekend had been in the 90s. Everyone seemed to want to escape to the waterfront.

The downside of the heat was I was going to have a hard time finding a place to park for the night that was both cool and safe. Last night, I'd barely been able to sleep because of the heat. I'd had to leave my door and flap open for airflow, which meant I kept waking up, thinking I heard someone outside.

And that wasn't even taking into account the mosquitos. I'd bought a mosquito net to sleep under, which kept them from mummifying me by drinking all my blood. It didn't stop the noise. The buzzing nearly drove me mad.

I pulled my faded map from a drawer. The online maps were

more current, but I couldn't mark them up with the best and worst spots.

My phone vibrated in its spot on the counter top. How had I managed to turn the ringer off again? At least I'd left it on vibrate this time. Dan had already called in his favor to GPS locate my phone once. Maybe for the sake of safety, I should set up a phone finder app and give him access. If Jarrod ever managed to find me and kidnap me, having something like that on my phone could allow Dan to find me in time to save my life.

Then again, anything that allowed someone to find me could be turned against me and used by Jarrod as well.

I nabbed my phone off the counter. Dan.

I swiped my finger across the screen. "I was just thinking about you."

I cringed. That sounded more flirty than I'd intended. I hadn't meant it to sound flirty at all.

"Where are you?" The noise in his background sounded like wheels on asphalt and forced air from an air conditioner.

His voice didn't have any of the teasing in it that I would have expected given my verbal slip.

"In my truck." Wow. Because that's what he meant. It was like that old joke my dad always found hilarious that asked where a dog bit someone and the man answered *On the corner of Elm and Fifth Street.* I couldn't even blame this on the heat. I'd experienced much hotter conditions before fleeing to Michigan. "At Clarkson Beach. I just sold out for the day."

"Stay there. I'm on my way."

He disconnected before I could ask any questions.

Something was very wrong.

My lungs closed up, and I couldn't get in enough air. I stumbled outside and over to the nearest picnic table. The shade was at least twenty degrees cooler than inside my truck. It hit me like an ice bath, and I sucked in a breath.

It couldn't be Janie or Claire. If anything happened to them, he wouldn't come to find me. He'd text me and tell me what hospital they were in.

That left two possibilities. Eve had been arrested, and he wanted to tell me in person.

Or Jarrod knew where I was.

That seemed like the most likely situation. Dan didn't want me driving my truck to him because it'd make me more conspicuous. If Jarrod was in Lakeshore, the more I moved around, the more likely he was to locate me.

I shoved my fingers into my hair. Him finding me was inevitable. I'd known all along that running would only prolong my life. I'd never be safe.

It wasn't fair that when I'd finally found people I cared about and I'd started to make my business a success, Jarrod would come in and take it all away from me again. I'd have no choice but to run. At least this time I'd have Dan to help me prepare for it. After all his years working undercover, he probably knew a lot about fake identities and changing appearances.

But Janie...and my business...

My stomach rolled, and I bent forward to put my head between my knees. I couldn't think about everything I'd be losing when I left here. It was my own fault for getting attached to anyone or anything in the first place.

Tires hit the gravel of the parking lot, and I straightened up. I couldn't risk that this was somehow Jarrod instead of Dan. I had to be ready to run.

Dan's car pulled toward me.

His movements when he got out were slow. Much too slow if this was an urgent situation where Jarrod might find me at any moment.

He motioned for me to sit back down at the picnic table. I hadn't realized I'd stood up.

I couldn't sit until I knew. "Is Jarrod here? In Lakeshore?"

Dan's eyebrows drew down. "What? No." He took my elbow and directed me back to the picnic table instead of waiting for me. "As far as I know, he still doesn't realize you're here."

My bones felt like they melted underneath my skin. I sank down. "What then?"

His expression was flat, but something flashed in his eyes that I couldn't read. Anger maybe? Or frustration? Something akin to one of those at least.

I felt like I was going to split apart. This made no sense. Maybe it was Eve after all. Maybe she had been lying to me this whole time.

Dan sat across from me like he had the first time we'd discussed a case together, back when he caught me trying to wheedle information out of the other food truck vendor who worked his grandfather's fatal birthday party.

"Detective Strobel received an anonymous tip as I was clocking out."

Dan's voice was so formal it sent a chill through my fingers. He'd thought Eve was guilty from the start. He wouldn't have been surprised. So this was concern for me? It didn't feel like concern. Wouldn't have concern had him sitting on the same side of the picnic table?

He locked his gaze on mine. "The person who called in thought you might be living in your truck, which is a health and safety violation. They suggested to Strobel that Anthony Rigman somehow found out about it and threatened you with reporting it as revenge for embarrassing him in public. The working theory is that you killed him to prevent that."

I sucked in a breath so hard that it hurt. So many thoughts swirled around in my head that it felt like someone had put my brain in a blender.

Someone either had to know about me living in my truck, or they guessed or they made it up as an attempt to deflect suspicion onto me, not knowing they'd actually hit on the truth. And now I was the primary suspect. Eve...please God let Eve not have been the one who did this.

I'd been poking around at Casa Bella Catering and at

the Rigman & Associates barbecue. Someone there might have gone looking for a way to shut me up and stumbled on my secret. It didn't have to be Eve. All it would have taken was for someone to feel threatened by me and then follow me around for a while to figure it out. It'd be clear after only a couple of nights that I didn't have anywhere else to go.

If there hadn't been a white glob on the picnic table that looked suspiciously like bird droppings, I would have put my head down.

This wasn't as bad as Jarrod finding me, but it came close.

My business was ruined. I'd have to pass a health-and-safety inspection and prove I wasn't living in my truck before I'd be allowed to stay open. I couldn't do that.

"Isabel?" The tone in Dan's voice said this wasn't the first time he'd called my name.

I forced myself to focus on his face. On his words. He was staring at me like he'd asked me something and was waiting for a reply.

"Isabel, are you living in your truck?"

He knew the answer already. He had to know the answer. He was a detective. He'd been an undercover police officer before that. As soon as the accusation came in, he'd probably put the pieces together and figured out it was the truth. Otherwise, he could have simply called me and told me about it.

Instead, he'd come here to confront me in person.

That look on his eyes that I hadn't been able to identity before. It was hurt. I'd hurt him by keeping it from him.

So much so that he'd come to me to confirm it rather than believing that I'd still been lying to him after everything he'd done to help and protect me.

"Yes." I squeezed the word out. "I've been living in my truck."

He stood up. The motion seemed abrupt. "Not anymore. We need to get all your personal stuff out of your truck before anyone comes to check on the tip, and then we need to find you a place to live."

If finding a place to live was that simple, I wanted to shout, *I would have done it months ago.* It wasn't like I enjoyed sweating it out in my truck in the heat or huddling under blankets next to a tiny space heater in the winter. I didn't enjoy jumping every time I heard a sound, wondering if someone was going to try to steal my truck with me in it. I certainly didn't enjoy not having a toilet in my "home." Or a shower.

I stuffed all that back down. Because I wasn't really angry at Dan. He'd been blindsided by this, and he was trying—again—to rescue me, even though I'd basically said I didn't trust him by withholding things from him.

No, I blamed Jarrod.

And myself. A little. Jarrod had forced me into running, but I could have told Dan the truth. He wouldn't have judged me. Looking back on it now, I wasn't even sure why I'd kept my living situation a secret.

But that didn't change the facts. "I can't rent an apartment. I don't have first and last month's rent. I don't have references. And I can't put my real name on a lease."

"Isabel." He said my name gently, in a way that made me think he'd forgotten it wasn't my real name. "I'm officially tampering with the investigation right now. This I could lose my job over, but if I don't do this, you could lose your job and a whole lot more. So please, grab up your stuff, put it in my car, and follow me to Claire's. We can talk about it more once we get there."

The fact that he told me to put my personal stuff in his car now instead of waiting until we got to Claire's made me think he was worried Detective Strobel might put a Be On the Lookout out on my truck. Had it come to that?

At the very least, Claire might let me pretend to be living with her. That was probably Dan's idea. I couldn't think of any other reason we'd be going to Claire's instead of to his place. I couldn't pretend to be living with him without opening him up to a lot of questions and speculation. Me living with him and Janie was less believable.

He probably wouldn't find it as funny as I did that the fake address I'd given to Detective Strobel was in Claire's neighborhood.

I went back into my truck. I didn't own much. I'd left the home I shared with Jarrod with only what I could carry to a church within walking distance. Since then, I hadn't acquired much. A pillow. A couple of blankets and my sleeping bag. My mosquito netting and space heater. A couple extra changes of clothes. My small bag of toiletries.

My folding chair and pop up table could stay. They weren't incriminating.

I brought it all out and dropped it into his trunk.

He slammed the lid. "That's everything? You're sure?"

I nodded again. What could I really say? I couldn't shake the feeling that I'd lost my best friend over this. The worst part was I hadn't even realized until I was dumping my meager belongings into his trunk that that's how I thought of Dan. He was my best friend. The best friend I'd had since my dad died.

He looked at me for a second more, then turned his back on me and climbed into his car. He drove away without waiting to see if I was following. Having some extra space between our vehicles was probably a smart idea anyway. If someone did pull me over, at least they wouldn't spot Dan and figure out that he'd warned me.

My eyes burned, but I wasn't sure whether it was over the rift I'd caused in our relationship or over the thought that my lies might actually cost him his job.

CLAIRE'S CAR WAS IN THE DRIVEWAY WHEN I PULLED UP, AND Dan had parked on the road, leaving me space to park in the driveway as well. That was the way it'd be if I actually lived here. He hadn't taken any chances.

He must have already taken my stuff and gone inside because neither he nor Claire were waiting for me by either car or out front.

That must mean they expected me to walk right in. Which made sense. If I did live here, I would walk right in. I might as well start playing the pretending game from this moment on or I could slip up when it mattered most.

I opened the door and stopped in the entryway to slide off my shoes. A man and a woman's voice, slightly raised but not yelling, came from upstairs.

"This is a terrible idea," Claire was saying.

"It solves both your problems," Dan replied.

I shouldn't be listening to this. Claire wasn't on board with Dan's plan, and that was only going to make me feel worse. Me being here could put her at risk of criminal conspiracy too. Though, if it came to that, I'd deny until my dying breath that she'd known about it.

"I'm..." I stopped. I was about to say *here*. Should I say *home*? I opted to finish with "Hello?" instead.

"Come on up," Dan called out.

Since they were sticking their necks out for me, I wasn't going to question it. It did show me one thing. Dan had no doubts about my innocence. If he had, he wouldn't have taken this risk, and he certainly wouldn't be bringing me in to live—

however temporarily—with the cousin who was like his second mother.

"We're at the end of the hall," Dan said as I was partway up the stairs.

I hadn't been on the second floor of Claire's home before. I passed what had to be the master bedroom, judging by the king-sized bed, and a second bathroom before reaching the room where they both were.

Claire held out something to me. I moved forward feeling like a robot being controlled by a remote.

A key.

"This is my spare that Dan had. I'll make him another one. I didn't have time after he called me. Make sure you put it right on your keychain."

She stopped talking, dipped her chin, and gave me a look that said *now*. I did as I was told.

"There are clothes in the closet. Hopefully I got the right size. No one was going to believe you lived here otherwise. Not even minimalists have less than a week's worth of clothing. And I unpacked your personal hygiene stuff into the bathroom."

Heat burned my face. I could think of few things more embarrassing than Claire picking through my personal hygiene items—unless it was Dan picking through them.

Claire had done a lot for a person who didn't want to go along with Dan's idea. It spoke to the closeness of their relationship. She really was like a mom watching out for her kid, even when he was grown. Dan had mentioned something about his mom dying young and his dad remarrying a woman he was never close with. It was no wonder Claire filled that role in his life instead. Without any children of her own, they would have naturally fallen together.

And now I was stepping into the center of it and putting them both at risk. "It'll only be for a short time. I'll be gone as soon as the Anthony Rigman case is closed."

They exchanged a wordy glance.

"Where will you go?" Dan asked.

I shifted my gaze away from his. It was a guilty move, but I couldn't seem to help it. The only honest answer was that I'd go back to my truck.

Dan took a step forward. His feet entered my line of sight. "Look at me please."

Even though it was a request, I didn't have the backbone to disobey. I looked up.

He was looking at me like he wanted to touch me but wasn't sure how I'd react. "You can't keep living in your truck. For a lot of reasons. Your locks are antiques. Anyone with access to the Internet could figure out how to break in. It's not even safe."

No. It wasn't. I'd seen so much during my time practically living on the streets that I knew it wasn't. Even more so for me. As proof of his point, when I was in Fair Haven, Nicole had even figured out how to break into my truck thanks to a video she'd watched.

But what did he want me to say. He couldn't possibly understand what he was asking. Something hot bubbled up in my chest. "It's not safe anywhere."

Claire's expression changed from one of mild annoyance to confusion.

Dan hadn't told her. Maybe she didn't know that my name wasn't Isabel Addington. I'd always assumed...

"Because of your husband?" Dan asked.

"Your husband?" Claire said at the same time as I said, "Yes."

She groaned. "I'm not sure which of you I'm more annoyed with right now." She glared at Dan. "Since you've obviously known this for a while."

Dan didn't look sheepish or even avert his gaze. "I did. It wasn't mine to tell." His gaze shifted back to me. "It still isn't."

They both focused on me. Neither of them said anything more.

Other than Nicole, it'd been a long time since anyone cared enough about me to press this way. To dig down into my business for my own good and put themselves in jeopardy for me.

Maybe you couldn't have true connection with people without that messy invasion, just like I couldn't make a cupcake without beating the eggs and the sugar together until they combined. Real relationships couldn't be surface conversations and pretending like everything was fine when it wasn't.

Besides, if I was staying here even temporarily, Claire deserved the truth.

I straightened my shoulders and tipped my chin up. Dan deserved the truth too. I'd been afraid that he'd believe Jarrod over me because Jarrod was a law enforcement officer, but Dan had proved that he wouldn't. He'd believe me and protect me.

"You're right to think me staying here is a terrible idea. I started going by Isabel when I left my abusive husband after he beat me so badly I lost our baby." My tongue stumbled over the word *abusive*. I couldn't remember if I'd ever said it out loud that bluntly before. "He's an FBI agent with resources and connections. I can't sign a lease because he'd find me. When he finds me, he'll kill me. He almost managed it once already since I left him. And I don't know what he'll do to anyone who gets in his way."

My throat closed up, and I couldn't have said anything more if I'd wanted to.

Claire let out a puff of air. She moved over to the bed and sat. "I need a minute to process all that."

For the first time since I'd known him, Dan looked like he didn't know what to say either. Since he'd learned I was trying to stay hidden from my husband—who he knew was also a law enforcement officer—he'd probably come up with a lot of reasons for why I was running. It looked like the real one hadn't crossed his mind.

He reached a hand toward me. I stepped back. He couldn't touch me right now. If he touched me, I'd break down.

"It's not for the reason you think," Claire said.

I jumped. She'd meant it literally when she said she needed a minute. It couldn't have been more than that.

I had no idea what she meant.

Claire was looking up at me. "My husband is refusing to give me a divorce, which means I'm not receiving alimony. I haven't been able to find a job because I've been out of the workforce for so long. Dan thought it would solve both our problems if you moved in and paid me rent. I'd have part of the income I need, and you'd have a home."

She stopped suddenly, like she hadn't meant to stay so much but once she started the words poured out.

"I didn't want you here because I didn't want you to feel sorry for me. It had nothing to do with the murder investigation."

The admission came out harsh, as if she was reprimanding me for something rather than confessing a failing on her part.

I didn't know what would be best to say, so I said the first thing that came to my mind. "I wouldn't have felt sorry for you."

"I see that now," she said without hesitation.

We stared at each other for a second.

Claire got up and brushed off her pants even though they were perfectly clean. "You're staying here. Neither of us should continue being punished for our poor choice in husbands. I think we've suffered enough."

Of all the people I would have guessed I'd form a kinship with, Claire hadn't been among them. "I think we have."

a pair of sunglasses slid across my truck's order counter where people usually passed cash to pay for their cupcakes.

I followed the arm back to where it attached to Eve, balancing on tiptoes so she could see me better. Her normally bubbly smile was absent. "You said you didn't have a pair. I thought these would look really nice with your face shape and complexion."

She hadn't come to my truck since I'd visited her at her office. I'd started to think she wasn't ever coming back. Now she showed up with a gift?

I picked the sunglasses up. They were trendier than I'd have selected for myself, but they were what I would have picked had I not constantly felt like I needed to blend in.

I turned them over in my hand. The brand name jumped out

at me from the arm. They were designer. Real designer. Not knockoffs.

I held them back toward her. "I can't accept these. They're too expensive."

Eve somehow managed to flip them around without ever taking them from my hand. "No, look."

She pointed at a tiny flaw in the left arm, almost like an air bubble got into the material while it was setting. You'd never feel it when you were wearing them because it was on the outside. It would make it so that people willing to pay this amount of money for sunglasses wouldn't want to buy them. If you were paying hundreds of dollars for a name brand, the product better be perfect.

"My brother works at the factory where they're made. He gets to buy ones that would otherwise be tossed for quality control reasons at a huge discount. Cheaper than you could get for a generic brand at a box store. Promise."

I wanted to slide them on. They looked like they'd give great coverage, so I wouldn't be randomly blinded like with my last pair. They also looked like they wouldn't pinch the way my last pair had. I'd constantly ended up with a headache at the end of a day from the way my dollar store pair pressed above my ears.

Eve glanced back over her shoulder. She'd been the only one in line, but now another couple approached.

She leaned closer. "Besides, they're an apology gift."

She had to be referring to how angry she'd seemed when I

asked about what in her past Detective Strobel could have found that would make her seem guilty. Her reaction had served to make her seem even more guilty. She had to know that. Was this gift meant to distract me?

The other customers had stopped in line behind Eve.

She stepped back and waved at me. "I'll see you later." She passed the couple and spun. She walked backward. "Her cupcakes are the best in the city. You won't regret it."

The cloud that had been temporarily blocking the sun moved, and I squinted.

I couldn't keep a gift long-term from someone who looked like she had killed her boyfriend, but Eve wasn't going to take the glasses back today. Whether she was genuine or not, I could at least wear them for now and give them back to her later.

I hated to even think it, but this gift made her seem more guilty, not less. She didn't want me to mull over her outburst.

I slid the sunglasses on, but my hand froze before I lowered it.

If Eve killed Anthony Rigman, then she might have been the one who called in the tip to the police about me living in my truck. I was around her enough that she could have figured it out, especially if she'd been following me, looking for a way to frame me.

Everything she'd done could be exactly what Dan suggested it might be—a way to stay close to the investigation and direct it. Even her "friendship" with me could fit that framework. Getting close to me meant it'd be easier to frame me. Or if I came up with another viable suspect to deflect attention from her, all the better.

I'd been gullible, just like Jarrod always said I was. He used to say he had to make all the decisions because I wouldn't know if someone was trying to trick me or not.

I served the customers who'd come up behind Eve and then closed down my flap even though I hadn't sold out completely. I didn't have the heart for selling anything more today.

I went back into my truck and sank down onto the floor. I pulled out my phone. I couldn't bear to tell Dan that I'd been naïve about Eve after all, but I needed to hear the voice of someone I knew I could trust.

I dialed his cell phone number.

"Just the person I was hoping to hear from," Dan said in lieu of a hello. "Would you be able to pick Janie up from vacation Bible school? I'm sorry to ask you to leave work, but Claire has a job interview."

His words doused the fire burning behind my eyes thanks to Eve's betrayal.

Even after what I'd told him, he trusted me enough to still take care of Janie. He trusted that I wouldn't let anything happen to her. "I'll head there now. Did you catch a new case?"

Dan was usually good about planning for someone to care for Janie in advance if he knew he'd be working late. His end of the call didn't have the normal noises I'd expect if he were driving, so he had to still be at the station.

"In a manner of speaking." He lowered his voice. "Strobel asked me to help with some interviews for the Anthony Rigman case. He found out that shortly before Rigman and his wife separated, the police were called in on a domestic disturbance. It turns out the receptionist I talked to at the barbecue actually filed and dropped a sexual harassment complaint against Rigman too. Strobel wants to talk to both women immediately, and since I'm the most familiar with the case apart from him, he's, surprisingly, asked for my help."

My stomach did a funny twist. Maybe I'd been too hasty in condemning Eve and believing what everyone else did about her. "Does this mean Eve's no longer a suspect?"

"Unfortunately not. Strobel will be talking to her as well. If he can prove that Rigman has a history of mistreating women and then bullying them not to report him, it speaks to motive. Strobel thinks Eve might have decided to solve the problem on her own rather than making a formal complaint where she might not have been believed."

I couldn't deny the ring of truth to what he said. So many women didn't report harassment, assault, and abuse because they feared they wouldn't be believed or that there'd be some negative repercussion. I was a perfect example.

While I couldn't condemn Eve if she'd felt backed into a

corner with no other way out, I couldn't condone what she'd done either. Assuming she was guilty.

The whole situation felt like a tangled web. I couldn't separate my friendship with her from her guilt. If she were guilty, she'd befriended me because I seemed like a vulnerable, easy target.

Ugg, I didn't want to spend any more time thinking about her or this case. With Dan actively involved now, it felt safer to back off and allow him to handle it. I had a little girl waiting for me.

The time had come to let the professionals handle it—something I never thought I'd hear myself think.

19

The man who came to the front of the line after a woman I recognized from the Rigman & Associates barbecue had a clerical look to him. His dress shirt was neatly pressed and his tie lay straight, at the perfect length for someone who'd tied it intending to wear it without a jacket. He had a clipboard tucked under one arm and a pen in his pocket.

He didn't look at my menu when he stepped up to the counter. "I'm here to conduct a health and safety inspection. Are you..." He glanced at the paperwork attached to the clipboard. "Isabel Addington?"

My tongue felt like it'd melted into the bottom of my mouth even though today was the coolest day we'd had in over a week. I nodded.

"Good. I'll need you to close up for about an hour."

The customers in line behind him had clearly heard what

he'd said. They turned away. Who knew if they'd come back. The first thing that most people thought of when a business underwent a health and safety inspection was that there was some violation. They wouldn't naturally assume that violation was me living in my truck. They'd think something like unclean equipment or rodents.

I flipped my menu board around. The backside read *Closed*. I'd never used it that way before because I generally shut my truck down and moved on.

I should have known the health and safety board wouldn't schedule an appointment. That would have given me a chance to hide any potential violations. Dan had been right to move fast. Not even a week had passed since Strobel received the tip about me living in my truck.

The inspector wanted to see my permits and asked me some questions, including my home address. I rattled off Claire's address. The man didn't give me a second look or pause. Either my lack of hesitation in giving my address already made him believe I wasn't living here, or he planned to check later. Or he might have already had the address I gave Detective Strobel. The number was only slightly off, something that could have been a mistake on Strobel's part.

The inspector went through every inch of the truck, including pulling open the compartment where I used to keep my sleeping bag and other personal belongings. If I hadn't had Dan's warning and the opportunity to move everything out, I'd be losing my license at that moment. With the advanced warning, I'd filled that spot with some decorative table clothes and a spare bag of flour.

He closed the storage compartment with a snap. His gaze shifted to the floor, and he stooped to pick up a piece of metal.

He handed it to me. "I could knock off a mark for cleanliness because of this, but everything else is in perfect order. I'll overlook it. You will need to make some upgrades to your truck within the next couple of years to stay within standards." He gave me his first smile since stepping up to my counter. He pulled a carbon copy of his check list off of his board and set it on my counter. "You have a nice day Ms. Addington. I'm sorry to have disturbed you for what was clearly a false call. We get them sometimes. Usually from competitors looking to cause trouble."

I almost offered him a cupcake on his way out, but that could have looked like I was trying to curry favor even though the inspection was over. Besides, he likely had some ethical guidelines that said he couldn't accept any sort of gift from a business he'd been sent to investigate.

I set the stone he'd handed me down on top of his report. It looked more like a piece of metal than a stone now that I was actually looking at it—silvery-white and shiny.

A picking at the back of my brain told me I'd seen something like it before.

My stomach twisted, and a numb tingle spread down both my arms. The tiny bit of metal looked like the pictures of antimony I'd seen online after Mark told Dan and I that antimony could have delayed the decomposition of Anthony Rigman's body to throw off the time of death.

I had to be sure.

I pulled out my phone and did an Internet search on antimony. The first article that came up told me what I already knew about antimony. Women in ancient Egypt used to use it as a cosmetic. High doses of it were fatal to humans. It was used in manufacturing glass, ceramics, and some plastics like those used in TV screens and sunglasses.

No picture.

My finger froze over the screen before I could tap back to check more links. Antimony was used in manufacturing sunglasses. Eve's brother worked for a company that made sunglasses. That's how she got the pair that rested on top of my head right now.

Had she really done this? All of this?

I tapped back. I had to make sure this was actually a piece of antimony that someone had planted in my truck before I jumped to any other conclusions.

The second link took me to a picture of a pound of antimony available for purchase from an online website. The image matched the stone on my counter perfectly.

Look, the part of me who didn't want to believe Eve had betrayed me said. *Anyone could have ordered antimony online.*

That was true. Unfortunately for me in one way. I'd have a

hard time proving I hadn't ordered antimony to kill Anthony myself.

I could take this piece and throw it away, toss it out my window while driving down the highway. I could stop somewhere and bury it. The inspector had found it, but he hadn't recognized what it was. No one knew about this but me.

Had that been the real purpose behind calling the health and safety inspector on me. Perhaps the person who'd done it hadn't actually known I was living in my truck. Maybe they hoped the inspector would take pictures of any "dirt" they found so that there'd be a record of antimony in my possession. Maybe they'd even thought the inspector might package up any unusual substances found.

Maybe they wouldn't take any chances, and they'd call the police with another tip soon. They might have gambled on the health and safety violation getting me out of my truck at night. With my truck empty for hours, they would have the opportunity to plant the antimony. This might have only been the first step. The police could be here with a warrant for a search next.

My brain felt too full of all the possibilities and options.

I had to calm down and figure out what to do with this stupid rock first of all. Throwing it away seemed short-sighted. The inspector might not have recognized it for what it was, but it also might not be the only one hidden within my truck. Whoever had done this couldn't possibly have thought a single piece—that could accidentally be knocked out of my truck or swept away—would be good enough. Likely there was more that I hadn't located.

I couldn't be sure that I would find it all. If Detective Strobel managed to get enough evidence together for a warrant, he might find a piece I'd missed.

Dan had found a solution when someone reported that I was living in my truck. He'd made sure that I got a place to live before the inspector showed up.

I dialed his cell phone number. He answered on the third ring.

"Holmes," he said, making it clear he hadn't looked at the screen before he answered.

"Someone planted antimony in my truck."

I kept my voice low even though no one was around to hear me. Who knew how loud his phone was. I didn't want anyone on his end to accidentally overhear. Having anyone at the police station find out would be the worst possible outcome.

There was a pause on Dan's end, almost as if I'd caught him off guard, and he needed to gather his thoughts before he responded. "Without touching anything, does it look like there's signs of a break-in?"

Without touching anything? I'd been touching it for hours, maybe even days, without realizing that something had been planted. I climbed out of my truck and checked all the doors and windows anyway. Everything looked normal. No obvious new scratches.

That wasn't good for me. "There's nothing that I can see. I don't even know when this happened. I'm not living in my truck anymore, so it's sitting unattended for hours."

I managed to keep my voice calm, even though everything inside me felt like it was pitching and turning. This case left me feeling out of control in a way I hadn't in a long time. I couldn't live in my truck anymore, which meant I wasn't ready to leave at a moment's notice. Someone had clearly gotten in. That person wasn't Jarrod, but it could have been him.

I wasn't safe here. I'd tried to tell Dan that, but he hadn't listened.

"Isabel?" Dan asked, as if he'd said something and I hadn't replied. "Are you still there?"

"I'm still here."

"I need you to come down to the station, okay?" His voice was unnaturally calm.

My heart beat so hard in my chest that it hurt. I'd explained to him about Jarrod. He knew Jarrod worked for the FBI. Surely he realized I couldn't walk into the police station with evidence that made me look guilty of a crime. They'd want my name. They'd want my fingerprints. They might even want my DNA.

This if what you get for trusting someone, Fear said.

I'd promised myself I wouldn't listen to Fear anymore. Too much of what he said had been drilled into me by Jarrod. I wanted Jarrod to have less control over my life, not more.

And yet, this time Fear might be right.

Why would Dan want me to come down to the station unless he now thought I was lying and might have been the one to kill Anthony Rigman? Nothing less could justify the danger I'd place myself in by coming.

I should have known what I had with Dan and Janie was too good to be true and couldn't last.

"Isabel?" Dan said again.

I'd have to leave Lakeshore. I couldn't take the antimony down to the police station. That's not what I'd been looking for when I called him.

But I couldn't tip him off to what I was planning.

"I need to close up, but I'll be there in about an hour."

"I'll meet you out front."

I knew if I'd said anything more than an hour, he'd have gotten suspicious. That meant I had about an hour and fifteen minutes to grab my stuff from Claire's house and get outside the city limits, heading for the Michigan border.

20

Thankfully, Claire's car wasn't in the driveway when I turned down her street. I'd expected to have to sneak past her, but she must be out at another job interview or grocery shopping. I'd contributed to this week's grocery bill. My chest tightened again at the thought that I wouldn't get to enjoy whatever she bought. Which was stupid. I was losing so much more in leaving. Not getting to eat a home-cooked meal anymore should be a small thing.

I jogged up the stairs. The less time I wasted, the better head start I'd have.

I collected my toiletries from the bathroom first, then threw my belongings back into my duffel bag. If I'd had a little more time, I'd have taken one last hot shower.

I didn't touch any of the clothes Claire bought me, even though I loved some of them. They had fit, and I'd been looking forward to wearing each item. Claire had bought those for me, and she didn't ask for any repayment, even though I now knew that her finances were almost as tight as mine.

Don't think about it, I admonished myself. *Don't think about showers, or real meals, or Dan and Janie and Claire. You have no other choice.*

I turned away before the burning in my eyes could turn to tears.

Claire stood in the doorway, a gardening trowel held out in front of her like a weapon. I dropped my bag and stepped back.

Claire lowered the trowel. "What are you doing? I thought an intruder was in the house. That maybe your husband..."

She'd come running up her with what was obviously the first thing she'd been able to lay her hands on to rescue me. And I was running away without even planning to say goodbye.

Claire's gaze drifted to my duffel bag. "What are you doing?" The suspicion in her voice was palpable.

She lunged forward, grabbed my duffel bag, and darted back as if she thought I'd try to snatch it out of her hands. She unzipped it.

Even if I'd tried to lie to her, she wasn't going to believe it. It was obvious I'd been sneaking out of the house while she was away.

The look she gave me was one I hadn't seen on Claire's face before. It reminded me of what I imagined she would have looked like had she come home to find I'd stolen something from her.

"Where were you going?" she asked. "The investigation isn't over, so don't try to tell me you were just moving back into your truck."

Even with her admonishment, I thought about lying. I was good at lying to angry people and not being caught.

The problem was I couldn't think of a reasonable lie to tell. She'd already crossed off the one I'd planned to use as unbelievable.

Instead, I told her about finding the antimony, calling Dan, and how he wanted me to turn myself in.

A line of wrinkles appeared between Claire's eyes. "Were those his exact words?"

I wasn't sure what she meant, so I shook my head and shrugged at the same time.

She set the duffel bag and trowel aside and frowned. "When you told him you found antimony in your truck, what, exactly, did he say? Did he actually tell you to turn yourself in?"

I frowned right back at her. "Dan's too good a detective to say that directly. He'd know I'd run if he did."

Claire slowly shook her head. "What, exactly, did he say?" she repeated slowly as if I was being belligerent on purpose.

Fine. I didn't want to shove past her, so the sooner this conversation was over, the sooner I could leave. As it was, Claire was likely going to call Dan as soon as I did. I might not be able to make it out of Lakeshore before a police officer spotted me.

"He asked me to bring the antimony down to the station. That's not word for word, but it's close."

I probably shouldn't have added that last part, but Claire's patronizing tone was getting under my skin. I wasn't Janie.

Her head shaking was emphatic now. "You assumed what he meant. Did you ask him if he suspected you now and wanted you to turn yourself in because it would go better for you with the district attorney?"

"Of course not. He—"

"Then you can't assume." Her hands went to her hips in a stance that reminded me too much of how she'd looked the first time we'd met in person, when she was blasting me for not bringing supplies to decorate my cupcake display at her grandfather's birthday party. "And you can't keep running away. Friends don't run away every time there's a misunderstanding. They work things out."

A misunderstanding. Was that possible? I'd heard Dan's words and tone of voice, but I'd been listening through the ears of someone who'd been betrayed by a man I loved and trusted. I'd married Jarrod expecting him to be one thing, and he'd showed himself to be another. And I'd still tried after that to fix things. For the longest time, I'd convinced myself that if I was different, he'd be better.

Maybe I didn't know how to have a healthy relationship or

to give people the benefit of the doubt. Maybe he'd broken something inside me that wouldn't heal the way my broken bones and bruises had. Did I still have the chance to change that about myself?

Claire's shoulders became even stiffer, and for a second, she looked like she regretted setting the trowel down because she'd like to have it in her hand to wave at me. "This is exactly what I've been afraid of. You're only thinking about yourself, and you can't do that anymore. Other people's hearts are involved now. Dan and Janie—"

Her voice cracked, and she waved her hand in the air as if I should be able to fill in the rest.

If I'd ever doubted that I mattered to Dan and Janie, I couldn't now.

My heart was involved too. Claire couldn't possibly know what it felt like to consider leaving Lakeshore. To consider leaving them.

But she was right. I hadn't considered what leaving would do to them. I had only been thinking about myself, about my heart.

She might also be right that I'd made an assumption about what Dan meant. Just like I'd assumed Eve was behind this based on sunglasses and her reluctance to blurt out her past.

My chest felt like it'd collapsed in. I couldn't take deep breaths. I'd face my fear and take the antimony to Dan at the station. I'd trust that he wouldn't have asked me to come if he didn't feel it was the right thing.

But first I'd go talk to Eve before I told my theory to Dan. She deserved that much for the friendship she'd shown me. Instead of leaving Lakeshore, I'd use what was left of my hour before I had to meet Dan swinging by Rigman & Associates. If I hurried, I could catch her before they closed. That's what a friend would do.

21

No one was in the reception of Rigman & Associates when I stepped into the door. The sign out front said they were supposed to be open until five o'clock, and it was only quarter to.

It didn't give me much time to work with, but I didn't want to call Eve after work. Despite Claire's lecture about giving friends a chance to explain themselves, I also didn't want to be foolish. If Eve had killed Anthony and I sounded like I knew too much, I didn't want hurting me to become a temptation. Approaching her at the office seemed like the safest option. Other people would be in the building.

Mr. Green bustled into the reception area, his face still looking like he'd gotten a bad sunburn. He grinned at me. "Isabel. It's so nice to see you again. Are you here about that quote or to visit Eve?" He waggled his eyebrows. "Remember, we'll give you the employee discount if you switch to us."

I could use that employee discount. Every amount of money I saved helped me have a better cushion for lean times. But first I needed to see Eve. If I had time after that before I had to meet Dan—which wasn't likely—I'd speak with Mr. Green about insurance. "Eve first."

He motioned me to follow him down the hallway. "You barely caught her. We're the last two left." We reached Eve's office, and he nodded down the hall. "I'll be one door down in case you change your mind about that quote."

I smiled at him in thanks. Knowing he was nearby settled my acrobatic stomach slightly. Not that Eve would have come to work today prepared to kill someone, but as Claire had pointed out to me, I had friends. I had people whose hearts would hurt if something happened to me. I had to protect myself for their sake, as well as for my own.

That truth didn't seem quite real yet. My brain bucked against it while my heart clutched it close. I had people who cared about me. I had people who thought I mattered.

It was time for me to move past thinking I didn't and couldn't.

That meant also exploring this friendship with Eve and asking for the truth.

"Are you coming in?" Eve asked, her tone teasing.

I poked my head around the corner and took a tentative step

inside. "You might not want me to once I tell you why I'm here."

The color left her cheeks, and she tensed.

I held up a hand in a *wait* gesture. "It's not about the case. Not directly." I took another step in. I had to commit to this. "I'm not good at trusting people, but I've started to think of you as a friend. Someone told me today that with friends you have to give them a chance to explain things that look bad rather than jumping to conclusions."

Spit it out, Isabel, I lectured myself. *You're only making this worse for both of you.*

Coming right out and asking her directly about something so personal, something that could prove she hadn't been my friend at all, made me feel like I was choking on something and couldn't free it from my throat.

The corner of Eve's eye twitched, and she closed her laptop. "You're still wondering why the police suspect me. The thing in my past."

I nodded because I couldn't manage anything else. Not for the first time, I wished I had Nicole's way with people. She would have found a less awkward means of doing this.

Eve rubbed at her shoulder like she was seeking some sort of pressure point to sooth herself. "It's because my mother-in-law has always been jealous of me. It's reached vendetta levels now."

My brain ground over the words. Eve was married. Honestly, if I were her mother-in-law and I knew she was cheating on my child, I wouldn't be thrilled with her either.

188 | EMILY JAMES

But I was making an assumption again. Eve didn't wear a wedding ring. "Widowed or divorced?"

Eve swallowed once. Twice. "Widowed. My husband died under what the police called suspicious circumstances." She made air quotes. "They eventually decided his death was an accident, but my monster-in-law could never accept it. Every couple of months she still goes to the police and asks them to re-open his case. She's convinced I did something to him even though I had nothing to gain and everything to lose. I lost everything."

Her voice tripped over itself, and she looked away, blinking rapidly.

No wonder she hadn't wanted to tell me. She'd lost the man she loved. Someone who'd been part of her family hadn't believed in her innocence. And that person continued to persecute her. To maintain her optimistic outlook on life, she couldn't dwell on any of that.

Eve forced her gaze back to my face. I could tell by how slowly she did it that it took effort. "Her accusations got worse after I started dating Anthony. She thought it was too fast. She didn't know what it was like going to work every day and having him pressure me for a date. I didn't want to date him at first. She and I never had the kind of relationship where I could have confided something like that in her."

Her words were rushing out now. I probably couldn't have stopped them if I'd tried.

"I think that's half the reason, other than fear of getting fired, that I stayed with him even after I learned what a dick he was. The more she pushed, the more I wanted to push back." She covered her face with her hands. "I should have told you when you asked the first time, but it's humiliating."

The one who should have been humiliated was her mother-in-law.

As soon as I thought it, it seemed like something I should say out loud. I'd held everything in for so long that my instinct was to keep it to myself, but a small nudging inside—God speaking to my spirit, my dad would have said—urged me to say it.

"The one who should be humiliated is your mother-in-law. The way she treated you was wrong."

Eve nodded but the movement lacked conviction.

I tensed, waiting for her to ask me in return why I was living in my truck. The silence stretched. Maybe she didn't know after all. If she didn't know, then that only confirmed that she hadn't been the one to make the call to the police.

But her brother did work in a place where he could have sourced the antimony for her. After all she'd been through, a brother seemed like the kind of person who would want to rescue her, whatever form that might take.

I needed to see her reaction. "Someone planted antimony in my truck."

Eve blinked rapidly as if she was working to focus back on me rather than staying lost in her memories. "What's antimony? Is it something that could hurt you?" Her eyes filled with tears, and she blinked so hard her eyelashes looked like butterflies trying to take flight. I hadn't noticed until then that they were fake. "If someone tried to hurt you because we were looking into Anthony's death, it'll be my fault. We need to stop."

If I were more like Nicole, I'd go over to her now and hug her or rub her back. But I couldn't convince my body to do it. Hugging and touching didn't come as naturally to me as they seemed to come to others. I couldn't even remember if I'd always been that way or if it was another consequence of how long I'd gone without kind touches.

I gave myself a mental shake. None of that was important right now. What was important was I'd been wrong to doubt Eve and think she was behind everything that had been happening. She didn't even understand the implications of the antimony. She'd jumped to the conclusion that someone tried to physically hurt me.

"Antimony is what was used to poison Anthony. Someone put it in my truck to make it look like it was me."

"Oh," Eve said, a touch of confusion in her voice. Then, with more understanding, "Ohhh." She got to her feet and sat back down like she wasn't sure what to do. "You know it wasn't me, right? Because your earlier question and now this. I didn't kill my husband or Anthony, and I wouldn't try to frame a friend even if I had."

A friend. Those words hit me in the chest and nearly knocked the air out of me. Even though I'd come in here and basically demanded to know if she'd done those very things, she still considered me a friend.

That, more than anything else, made me sure she was innocent.

I hadn't been a very good friend to her up to this point. In fact, right before someone reported me to the police, I'd been close to giving up on the case because Dan assured me I wasn't being seriously considered as a suspect.

"I know you weren't behind it." At last, I did. I wouldn't let anyone or anything shake that again. "I'm heading to the police department right now to give them the antimony I found. They'll probably start checking to see if anyone who had a motive to kill Anthony also managed to buy or otherwise procure antimony."

Eve's hand didn't so much as subconsciously twitch toward the sunglasses lying on her desk. She truly didn't know anything about antimony, not even that her brother's job could make her seem even more guilty than she already seemed.

If the police arrested her, I'd give her Nicole's number. Until then, I wouldn't stop trying to find out who'd really killed Anthony.

"Sorry to interrupt," Mr. Green said from the doorway, "but didn't you say you needed to leave on time today?"

Eve picked up her cell phone and glanced at the screen. "I didn't know it was so late. Oil changes wait for no woman." Some of her perkiness was back in her voice, but it sounded more forced than usual. She looked to me. "Want to walk out with me?"

"Actually, I wanted to borrow her for a minute." Mr. Green dabbed at his forehead with an old-fashioned handkerchief. He held up a hand before I could say that I had another appointment. "I won't keep you long. I took the liberty of making up a quote for you—just in case. I'll give it to you so you can look it over."

I was supposed to meet Dan in ten minutes now, but it'd likely be faster to accept the quote than it would be to argue with him. I nodded and waved for Eve not to wait for me. Neither of us had time to chat in the parking lot anyway.

I followed him back to his office. "Just one minute. I have it ready." He rifled through some papers on his desk, then pretended to smack himself on the forehead and moved over to the filing cabinet in the corner. "I didn't mean to eavesdrop, but did I hear you say the police think someone is trying to frame you for Anthony's murder?"

Something cold slithered up my spine and wrapped around my throat. He'd said he had the papers ready, so why would they be in the filling cabinet? Unless there were no papers or he was stalling. Unless he'd drawn me in here to see what I knew about Anthony's murder.

Mr. Green had as good a motive as anyone for wanting Anthony gone. He'd been stuck in a partnership with a man who couldn't have been more the opposite of him. He either didn't have the money to buy him out or Anthony wouldn't sell. Considering the business was called Rigman & Associates rather than Rigman & Green or even Green & Associates, Mr. Green must have either been a minority partner or became a partner later. It explained why Anthony prevented him from doing things he otherwise would have wanted to do, like give a good recommendation to Harper. There may have even been a clause in their contract that stopped Mr. Green from selling his half and starting over without Anthony's approval. Many contracts had non-competes these days.

Everyone spoke well of Mr. Green. He seemed to try to be even kinder to make up for Anthony.

Maybe he'd found himself trapped and finally couldn't stand it anymore. Killing Anthony—wrong as it was—might have seemed like the only way to protect his business and his employees from a man he hated.

If I were right, I couldn't let Mr. Green know I suspected him.

I edged backward toward the door slowly so as not to draw his attention. "I'm actually supposed to be meeting with a detective right now. He didn't give me a choice. I'll come back for the quote another day."

"I'm really sorry, Isabel."

I started to tell him not to worry. That I could return for the quote anytime. Until I looked up and saw the gun pointed at me.

22

"You know that I didn't want it to come to this." Mr. Green moved around his desk, keeping the gun pointed at me. "I'd hoped the police would simply arrest you, and we could put this all behind us. But I can't have them looking into my buying history."

He held the gun with one hand, as if he'd gleaned his technique from TV. Jarrod used to rant at shows and movies constantly where people did that. Anyone with training used two hands on their weapon. It gave more stability, which in turn helped with better aim.

Maybe I could use that. If I dove at him, maybe his shot would go wild.

Then again, *wild* didn't mean it wouldn't hit anything vital. It only meant the bullet wouldn't go where he intended it to go.

Frankly, I didn't want to trust where the bullet would land even if he aimed for a non-vital part.

But he wasn't likely to aim for a non-vital part if he shot that gun. He wouldn't have pulled it on me if he intended to let me live. He hadn't gone to all this work only to have me ruin it.

"Close the door." His words were so soft that my mind couldn't make them fit the situation. "And then put your cell phone on the desk."

I stepped backward toward the door. Frontward would have made it easier for me to run, but backward meant he had to continue looking me in the face. His hand on the gun shook slightly. He wasn't a hardened killer. He'd probably bought that gun, realized he couldn't shoot Anthony, and then poisoned him instead.

I couldn't bank on him not being willing to shoot me now, though. He'd killed once already. In elementary school, I'd gone on a field trip to a homestead farm, and one of my classmates asked the farmer how he could kill and eat his pigs. He'd said the first time is the worst, and that every time after that got easier. I assumed the same was true for killing people.

If I ran and he was willing to shoot me, he'd have an easy shot. The hall was long and narrow. He could empty his gun, and one of the shots was bound to hit me.

As long as I was alive, there was still hope of talking him out of this. If I ran and he shot me, it was all over.

I reached back, found the door, and closed it.

I moved forward at a pace that would have allowed a snail to beat me in a race. Giving up my phone felt worse than closing the door. My phone was my only hope of calling for help.

I stopped a foot away from his desk. His gun pointed at the large target of my torso. I tried not to look at it.

Instead, I forced myself to look him in the eyes. Everyone said he was a good man. Maybe I could reason with him. "I know you don't want to do this. You'll be a hero to most of your employees for freeing them from Anthony, but I'm innocent. You're not the kind of man who would hurt an innocent woman."

His gun didn't lower, but he patted the air with his free hand, as if he would have patted me on the shoulder had I been closer. "You and Eve stirred up trouble by refusing to leave this all alone. I wouldn't have had to otherwise. You were only supposed to go to prison for this. It would have been better for you than living in your truck. I knew that as soon as Eve mentioned it the last time you were here."

"Eve didn't say I was living in my truck." I modulated my voice to the same kind of tone late night radio DJs used. Soft, soothing, lower pitched. The kind of tone that was meant to help people relax. "She said I practically live there because I spend so much time there. I live in a house."

A micro frown passed over his features. So he hadn't actually known I lived in my truck. He'd misunderstood Eve, and he'd run with it. He'd convinced himself he'd be helping me. Prison, to his way of thinking, was warm in winter and cool in the summer. I'd have regular food and indoor plumbing. He must have thought that was a good trade-off for my freedom.

"This doesn't have to go any further." I took a step back toward the door again. "The police don't suspect you. They suspect Eve, and they won't be able to tie her to the antimony."

That wasn't entirely true with her brother's job, but hopefully he didn't know that.

His gaze glazed over slightly, and he didn't stop me as I took another step toward the door. "It's too risky," he said almost to himself. "If they can't find the connection between her and the antimony, they'll look at the rest of us."

His hand tightened on the gun. I froze.

He motioned with his free hand toward the desk. "I said put your phone down. And take a seat. I've come too far and done too much to protect this business to risk it all now."

The softness was gone from his voice, replaced by a hard resolve. I felt like I was getting a glimpse of what he must have looked like when he spiked whatever Anthony ate or drank with the antimony. Nothing I said was going to convince him to turn back.

I laid my cell phone on the desk, edged around, and sat in his swivel chair. It smelled a bit like pipe tobacco and the leather on the arms was worn thin.

I'd always thought that, if I died young, it'd be by Jarrod's hand. I hadn't thought it would be because I'd stepped in to help a friend and got in over my head.

Mr. Green pocketed my phone. "I'm going to get rid of your truck, and then I'll come back for you. The police will think you ran away. They'll stop investigating the rest of us and look for you instead."

He glanced back at the door. If I'd realized what he was doing one second quicker, I might have been able to launch myself over the desk and take him down. Or at least put up a good fight.

But he was looking at me again before I came up with a plan.

"This door can be unlocked from the inside." He spoke as if he were talking to himself. Then he jabbed the gun toward me slightly as if it were a sharp-edged weapon rather than a projectile one. "Get up. We're going to the storage room."

He stepped back so that I couldn't easily reach for the gun while I passed. He pressed it into my back once I was in front of him.

Even he couldn't miss from that range, one-handed grip or no.

"I promise that when the time comes to end this, I'll make it quick." His voice had an edge of penitence, but not enough that he might change his mind. More like a vegan putting out mouse traps. "If you believe in God, I'd suggest you spend your last minutes praying rather than trying to break out. There's no window, and the wall butts up to a building that's empty for the night. Even the janitorial staff won't be in until the weekend."

He had me open a door and step inside. Before I could turn around, he slammed the door behind me, and there was the grate and rattle of a key in the lock.

I spun around. The doorknob was the old-fashioned kind without any way of unlocking the door from this side. That had to be some sort of building code violation.

Not that I'd have the chance to report it if I died today.

He'd said he was going to take my truck and get rid of it. Maybe I should have signed up with his insurance company. At least then anything he did to my truck, they'd have to pay out.

Of course, if I were dead, there'd be no one to make the claim.

He hadn't taken my keys from me, which meant he already had a set. That explained how he'd planted the antimony in my truck without leaving any signs of forced entry.

He must have filched them at the barbecue. I'd left the truck unlocked and the keys on the driver's seat. Dan, Claire, and I were going in and out gathering food, and I'd wanted either of them to be able to move the truck if need be. I hadn't expected anyone to steal from the truck or to steal the truck in those circumstances.

No one would have been keeping tabs on Mr. Green. He could have easily slipped to a hardware store to copy my keys. My truck didn't have a built-in alarm, and it was old enough that the ignition key didn't have those electronic chips that made keys impossible to copy in newer vehicles.

I pressed the heels of my hands to my eyes. None of that mattered now.

What mattered was finding a way out before he returned.

He'd been telling the truth about the room not having any windows. The back wall was actually made out of brick, so I couldn't even bang on it in the hope he'd been lying about the business next door.

The walls were lined with tall, grayish filing cabinets that looked a decade older than me. Everything about the room said "outdated" and didn't match with the front-of-the-business appearance. Even the air conditioning duct above me was double-sized, and the air coming out in an icy blast rattled the grate.

I moved over to the door and inspected the doorknob. The screws were on the outside, so I couldn't even try to use my truck key to take the doorknob off. I didn't know how to pick a lock, and he'd taken my phone, so I couldn't search the Internet for a solution. Of course, if I'd had my phone, I wouldn't need to search for how to pick a lock.

My brain wasn't thinking clearly.

There wasn't even anything in the room heavy enough for me to smash at the doorknob with to try to knock it off, and the door itself was made of metal.

My legs felt wobbly, like they'd already given up hope.

I could not give up. If I did, Claire would think I'd run

anyway. Worse, Dan would think I'd run. And how would either of them explain my sudden absence to Janie?

It'd been one thing when disappearing was my choice. It was another thing entirely when someone else took that choice from me. I'd had enough of my choices stripped from me.

Another blast of frigid air hit me, and I shivered. I glared up at the air duct.

And froze.

That air duct was huge. Human-sized huge.

I wouldn't have been able to fit into a newer heating or cooling duct. They'd started making them smaller in the last twenty years.

This duct looked like it'd almost been original to the building. The hole coming into the room, at least, was large enough that I could fit through it. Even if I hit a blockage further along and couldn't get all the way out, Mr. Green couldn't shoot up the entire ceiling in the hopes of hitting me. Not only would that require a lot of bullets, but it'd be sure to draw attention. It'd sounded like he planned to take me away from here before killing me to avoid that very thing. Otherwise, he could have shot me before getting rid of my truck.

Worst case, I got stuck in there. Once Monday came, I could scream until someone called the police. At least I'd be alive to scream.

First, I had to get up to the grate. I stood under it and jumped. My fingertips didn't even brush the metal.

I circled the room. No ladder. Not even so much as a step stool. The only things in the room other than me were the filing cabinets. If I tipped one over, it might be enough.

I moved to the cabinet that looked like it would fall closest to the grate. I pushed against it. It barely moved. It must be full from top to bottom with records.

Getting rid of my truck couldn't take that long. Mr. Green could be back any minute. I had to hurry.

I ripped open the bottom drawers and tossed the file folders out. That should help make it top-heavy as well.

I pushed again. It moved slightly this time. I put my shoulder into it and rocked. It gained momentum and finally tipped. It landed with a crash that felt sharp in my ears. If the floor hadn't been concrete, I would have sworn I felt it shiver.

It wasn't perfectly aligned with the grate, but it was close.

I scrambled on top. The metal gave slightly beneath my feet. If I jumped and missed or wasn't close enough to grab hold, I might fall right through. The last thing I needed was to create my own version of a snare, impaling myself on rusty metal.

I wouldn't be able to jump to test it. I reached my hand up. The tips of my fingers grazed the grate. I was so close. And still so far away.

If I got out of here alive, I wasn't ever going to consider running from Lakeshore again. Not seriously anyway. All I wanted right now was to give Janie a hug, sit across the table from Dan and see him smile, and be lectured about something small and stupid by Claire.

I had to get out of here alive. As Claire had pointed out, my heart wasn't the only one at stake. I had people who cared about me.

I stepped down from the filing cabinet. I couldn't knock another one over in such a way that it would get me closer. I'd have to try to pull a drawer from one of the remaining cabinets.

I sprinted to the closet cabinet and yanked the middle drawer open. It caught before coming free.

But most cabinets had removable drawers, didn't they? Or was that only newer versions and not dinosaurs like these?

In the filing cabinet I had back when I had a house, the drawers came out when you tilted them back and lifted slightly to take them off their tracks. I tore the paperwork out of the drawer and tried it. It gave slightly but didn't release.

I tugged harder, bracing my foot against the bottom of the cabinet. The drawer let go, and I flew backward. The drawer screeched across the floor. I landed hard, my wrist twisted under me, and pain shot up my arm.

No! If I broke something in my wrist, I wouldn't be able to climb up into the ducting even if I reached the grate.

I crawled to my knees and gently rotated my wrist. Spikes of pain shot through it, but I could still move it, and it didn't look like anything was broken. I could work with a fracture. Fractures didn't kill people. I'd had them before.

I turned my mind away from the pain and placed the drawer on top of the prone filing cabinet. The metal front looked even thinner than the main body of the cabinet. I wouldn't have long once I stood on it.

I craned my head back for a better look. I couldn't see screws on the grate. It almost looked like it rested in a slot. If so, I'd need to shove it back into the vent and then haul myself up before the cabinet gave out.

I waited for a couple of minutes, even though every creak of the vents above me made me jump, thinking Mr. Green had returned. I needed to give my wrist as much of a chance to rest as possible.

When I couldn't stand waiting any longer, I stepped up onto the main cabinet. It groaned under my weight.

I'd have to do this in two stages and pray the old pieces of cabinet could hold out long enough.

I planted one foot onto the drawer, raised my hands over my head, and pushed off. My hands collided with the grate, and I shoved. It was heavier than I'd expected, and slightly rusted shut. My wrist burst into internal flames, but the grate clattered to the side. I'd have to go the other way when I jumped in.

The drawer beneath me let out a popping noise. I lowered to the main cabinet and stumbled back to the ground.

One of the screws in the drawer had given out. I wouldn't be able to hesitate once I climbed on again. I'd have to grab the edge of the ducting and jump up without hesitating.

Blood pounded in my wrist. If it'd been fractured, I'd made it worse. But I was almost there. I just had to get inside and I'd be safe. Safe-ish. Safer than I was now anyway.

I drew a deep breath, stepped back up on the main cabinet, and counted to three. I launched onto the drawer, grabbed the edge of the ducting, and jumped. I pulled up with my arms.

My wrist felt like it exploded and black dots flashed at the edges of my vision. I got my elbows over the edge, then my stomach up onto it. I wriggled and pulled until I lay on my side inside the ceiling.

The ducting moaned but held. I hadn't considered that it might not be able to bear my weight.

I needed to crawl farther down the ducting so that my feet weren't dangling over the edge, but waves of nausea buffeted me every time I tried to lift my head. I couldn't feel my fingers anymore on my injured hand. Everything from my wrist down was heat and pain.

Move, a voice in my head shouted at me. *You didn't come this far to give up now.*

It didn't sound like Fear this time. Fear had been quiet this whole time when he normally would have been beating me into a panic attack.

This time the voice I heard urging me on sounded like a combination of Claire and Dan.

I closed my eyes and imagined Claire with her hands planted on her hips, lecturing me about how quitters never prosper. I imagined Dan, going on with his life, refusing to let everything he'd lost and been through beat him. I imagined Eve, sunglasses on her head and smile on her face, choosing joy. And I imagined Janie, her little forehead screwed up in concentration, refusing to give up as she struggled to figure out the Russian piping tips.

They weren't quitters, and neither was I.

I breathed in through my nose and out through my mouth and inched my way deeper into the ducting. Dust filled my nose and made my eyes itch. The ducting swayed beneath me.

Definitely not safe. Had this been new, light-weight ducting, or the kind of ducting they put into houses, it never would have supported my weight.

I hit a portion that felt more solid and stopped. I had to be over top of the wall now that separated the filing room from the hallway.

I laid my head down and closed my eyes. There was nothing else I could do but wait.

23

I dreamed that Dan was calling my name.

No, it couldn't be a dream. There was no way I could have fallen asleep with the pain. Maybe I'd passed out.

I forced my eyes open, but nothing met my gaze. Everything around me was dark. This wasn't my truck. Where was I?

Mr. Green pulling a gun on me and then my struggle to climb up into the ceiling came back in a rush.

"Isabel?" Dan's voice called again. "Are you in here?"

I tried to call back, but my tongue felt taped to the floor of my mouth.

"Check all the closets and every locked room," Dan was saying. His voice sounded muffled.

Which made sense. We did have ceiling tiles and metal duct-work between us.

The pain was muddling my thinking.

I swallowed hard, trying to moisten my mouth. "Dan!"

His name came out in a croak. Maybe I was dreaming after all, and it'd be one of those dreams where you screamed for help but no one heard you.

I tried again.

"I hear her," he said. "Isabel?"

His voice was louder than the first time. He must have moved closer.

"I'm up here." The words came easier now. My brain and my vocal cords were syncing up again.

"Up where?" Dan's voice had stopped moving.

I didn't blame him for being confused. Murderers didn't tend to leave their intended victims in the ceiling. I tapped on the edge of the duct with my good hand. It clanged. "Up here. But you might want to call the fire department. I'm pretty sure I can't get out."

Everything between then and when I woke up in my room in Claire's house was a bit of a blur. Dan did radio for the fire department, and they had to cut through the ceiling and the ductwork to get me out.

I must have passed out again because the next clear memory I had was of a doctor saying my wrist was badly sprained but not broken, splinting it, and prescribing me some strong pain killers and an ice pack.

I couldn't remember how I'd gotten from the hospital back to Claire's and then into bed. A few times I thought I heard a child's voice saying something about pigs and chickens and little red trucks. The only way I could explain that was the pain medication.

I opened my eyes slowly. The room around me was muted, like it was daytime, but someone had drawn the curtains to block out some of the light. My wrist rested propped on a pillow on a partially melted ice pack.

And Janie's face was less than a foot away.

I jerked back into my pillow slightly.

She grinned. "She's really awake this time," she yelled.

She was so close to me when she did it that my ears rung with it, and I could smell peanut butter, grape, and milk on her breath. I wouldn't have cared if she smelled like garlic and sweaty feet. Seeing her again made so much of my world right again.

I motioned her over and wrapped my good arm around her.

She clung to me like an adorable tick. "I wanted to stay on the bed with you like Claire does for me when I'm sick, but Daddy said I couldn't because I might hurt your wrist on accident. He put the chair for me instead. I read to you." She pointed to a book with the title *Farmer Doug's Big Red Truck*. "It's the only one I know, so I read it lots."

So it hadn't been a hallucination after all. "Thank you. I'm sure that's why I had good dreams."

She let go and pointed to a very drippy cup on the bedside table. The residue inside was a faded purple. "I made you a purple cow too. But then the ice cream started to melt, and I got thirsty, so I drank it. I'll make you another one now that you're awake."

She darted from the room.

Dan ducked in after her, barely avoiding being run over when she barreled past.

"What's a purple cow?" I whispered.

Dan's smile looked more relaxed than I'd seen in weeks. "Grape juice, ice cream, and milk. She learned how to make it at vacation Bible school. She wanted to make you something herself, and that's really the only thing she knows how to make without help." The smile faded from his face, and he took the chair Janie had vacated. "You might need the sugar hit once you hear the rest of what I need to tell you."

Part of me wanted to tell him that I wasn't ready for any bad news yet. But the more rational part knew I wouldn't be able to rest until I knew. "Did Mr. Green get away?"

Dan shook his head. "We caught him, and he gave himself up immediately. He kept defending his actions to anyone who would listen, saying he did it to protect his employees."

Because of my negative experiences, I'd lean more toward vigilante justice if someone didn't check me. Mr. Green was a perfect example of the problems inherent in not having a dedicated police force. He'd found a way to justify everything he did, even harming me, an innocent bystander, in pursuit of the greater good. He'd sacrificed the few to save the many.

Having seen the ways an individual taking justice into their own hands could go wrong, and having now met individuals like Dan and Nicole's friends in the Fair Haven police department, I think I was safely content with the justice system handling things. Flaws and all, it was better than the alternative.

There was one part of all of this that I hadn't been able to work out. "How did you find him? I thought I was the only one who'd figured out he was Anthony Rigman's killer, and I didn't realize it until it was too late."

Dan's foot bounced on the floor. "You didn't show up at the station, and you didn't answer when I tried to call you."

No, I hadn't. For obvious reasons. "I guess you could say I was locked up."

My wrist still hurt a bit too much for me to grin along with my joke.

Either Dan didn't catch the play on *I was tied up* or he was worried about my reaction because his cheeks didn't even twitch with the start of a smile.

"I don't want you to think I'd do this if I wasn't worried about your wellbeing."

I understood. He'd tracked my phone again the way he had when he'd thought Jarrod might have found me. "It'd be stalkerish if you did it just to ask me to come over for dinner, but any time you think my life might be in danger, feel free."

The tension was still in his shoulders. "I didn't think your life was in danger this time."

Oh, wait. He'd thought I was running. As much as I hated to admit it, in some ways, it amounted to the same thing. "Someone once told me that I'm safer where I have friends."

His smile crinkled the corners of his eyes. "Sounds like a smart man."

"He is." He shouldn't have been hesitant to tell me anything of what he had so far. More was coming. "I'm still waiting on the bad news."

"Your truck. When we found Green..."

My stomach clenched, and I was suddenly glad I hadn't put Janie's purple cow in it yet. "What did he do to it?"

Dan drew in a deep breath. "If I hadn't found him by tracking your phone, the fire department would have. He took it to an isolated spot outside of town and doused it in gasoline. If we'd been much later, I might not have even recognized it."

Buzzing filled my ears. The truck hadn't technically been my home anymore, but it still felt the same as if I'd watched my house burn down. Only worse. I'd lost my home and my business.

Warm fingers closed around mine. I glanced down. Dan's hand held mine. The panic brewing in my chest blew away rather than turning into a storm.

"Do you have insurance?" he asked.

I couldn't help it. It felt so ironic that an insurance salesman caused me to need my insurance. I cracked up laughing.

"Isabel!" Janie zipped into the room and plopped a glass of thick purple goo on the counter. "Your friend's here. She's coming up, and I'm going to make her a purple cow too."

"Did you call Nicole?" I asked Dan.

He shook his head.

Eve stepped into the room, her sunglasses pushed up on top of her head. She glanced back over her shoulder. "Did she just call me a cow?"

Maybe it was the stress, but I broke out laughing again. This time both Dan and Eve joined me.

When we pulled ourselves together, Dan gave up his chair to Eve.

She dropped into it and pulled a tablet out of her oversized purse. "I won't stay long, but I made you a little gift. I wanted to thank you for sticking with me through all of this."

At least if it was a gift she'd made, I wouldn't worry about the cost. Not like the sunglasses.

I edged up in the bed until I could sit up straighter.

She tapped on the screen a couple of times, then handed the tablet to me.

On the screen was the website for a catering business. The color scheme was pink and purple, like my truck had been. The design was beautiful without sacrificing function.

I knew what she'd done before my eyes found the website name—How Sweet It Is.

Eve leaned forward. "I heard what happened to your truck, but if you have a website, you can still take catering orders and cook from the kitchen here."

Tears burned at my eyes. Her gift was thoughtful. It would help grow my business.

It was also more dangerous than she could ever know. Because someone at the Rigman & Associates barbecue had obviously been taking pictures. The website was full of images of me, Dan, Claire, and my truck.

My truck was gone, and the insurance money might or might not be enough to buy me another one. I'd only been able to afford the most basic coverage. So Jarrod couldn't come looking for my truck.

But my face was everywhere.

If I hadn't already decided I wasn't going to run anymore, I'd be gone, truck or no truck.

"Do you like it?" Eve asked, her voice uncertain.

My throat felt too thick to speak. I nodded and handed her tablet back to her.

She grinned. "I can help you keep it updated or show you how to do it yourself. It's hosted through my sister's company, and she owed me a favor, so you have five years of free hosting." She sneaked a glance at the glass of melting purpleness of my bedside table. "And now I'm going to get out of here before I have to taste whatever that is."

"It's actually pretty good," Dan said.

Eve scurried to the door. "I'll take your word for it."

She wiggled her fingers at me in a wave and was gone.

Dan came back to my bedside and pulled the website back up on his phone. His gaze scanned the screen. "We can take the pictures down. I have enough tech skills to do it without Eve knowing about it unless she goes back and looks."

Eve wasn't likely to look. This project was complete. She'd be on to the next one.

The blood seemed to pound through my sprained wrist with extra force. "It might already be too late. He might already know I'm here."

Dan laid his phone down and took my hand again. "If he does, we'll face him together. Remember, that's what friends do."

RECIPE: RED VELVET CUPCAKES

I first learned to bake red velvet cake when I met my husband. I'd never even heard of it before. (I guess it's more common in the US south?) My husband's birthday tradition, though, was to have red velvet cake, so I knew I had to figure it out. These cupcakes were born out of that. They're less dense than the cake version, but they still have that traditional red velvet flavor.

(And if you don't like to use food coloring, you can leave it out. The only thing it changes is the color.)

Cake:

1 cup granulated sugar

6 tablespoons vegetable oil

1 large egg, at room temperature

1/2 cup buttermilk, at room temperature

1 teaspoon vanilla extract

1/2 oz red food coloring

1/4 cup hot water

1/2 teaspoon white vinegar

1 cup all-purpose flour

1/2 teaspoon baking powder

1/2 teaspoon baking soda

1/2 teaspoon salt

1 tablespoon cocoa powder

Cream Cheese Icing:

1 (8 oz) package cream cheese, at room temperature

1 1/2 cups powdered sugar

1 1/2 cups heavy whipping cream (35%), cold

1/2 teaspoon vanilla extract

INSTRUCTIONS

To Make the Cake:

1. Preheat the oven to 350 degrees F, and line a muffin tin with cupcake liners.

2. In a large bowl, beat together sugar and oil until well combined.

3. Add in the egg, and beat until well combined. (You'll know you've reached that point because the mixture will look smooth and uniform in color.)

4. Mix in buttermilk, vanilla extract, and red food coloring. Combine well.

5. Mix in hot water and vinegar until well combined.

6. In a medium bowl, whisk together flour, baking powder, baking soda, salt, and cocoa powder. These are your dry ingredients.

7. Add your dry ingredients to your wet ingredients and gently mix by hand until just combined.

8. Fill the cupcake liners 2/3 full with the batter.

9. Bake for 18 minutes or until a toothpick inserted into the center comes out clean. (It's okay if there are bits of cake stuck to the toothpick, but not wet batter.) Do not overbake.

10. Allow to cool in the pan for 5 minutes, then remove to wire rack to finish cooling.

To Make the Icing:

11. Place your bowl and mixer whisk attachment into the freezer for 10 minutes.

12. Remove whipping cream from fridge at the same time as you remove them from the freezer.

13. Immediately, whip the cream on high speed until thick and fluffy, about 1-2 minutes.

14. In a separate bowl, beat together cream cheese and powdered sugar. Once they are well combined, add in the vanilla extract and continue to beat until it's combined as well.

15. Fold the whipped cream into the cream cheese mixture.

16. Store cupcakes in the refrigerator. Bring to room temperature before eating.

Makes 12 cupcakes.

LETTER FROM THE AUTHOR

*T*hank you for continuing on with Isabel, Dan, Claire, and Janie.

I love Isabel as a character because she has so much room to grow. What happened to her in the past isn't fair, but she hasn't let it stop her. She's trying to figure out a way to have a better life.

For those of you who are fans of the Maple Syrup Mysteries, I hope you also enjoyed the cameo by Nicole and Mark.

The next book in the Cupcake Truck Mysteries is *Gum Drop Dead*, where a body falls from the sky at a hot air balloon festival!

If you want to know when the next Cupcake Truck mystery releases, make sure to sign up for my newsletter at www. subscribepage.com/cupcakes.

And if you enjoyed this book, I'd really appreciate it if you'd leave an honest review on Amazon or Goodreads. Reviews help fellow readers know if this is a book they might enjoy. Even a short sentence helps!

Love,

Emily

MAPLE SYRUP MYSTERIES

Looking for something to read until the next Cupcake Truck Mystery comes out? Try Emily James' Maple Syrup Mysteries. This thirteen book series is complete and available in both print and ebook formats. The first four books are also available as audiobooks.

Criminal defense attorney Nicole Fitzhenry-Dawes thought that moving to the small Michigan tourist town of Fair Haven and taking over her uncle's maple syrup farm would keep her far away from murderers, liars, and criminals. She couldn't have been more wrong...

If you love small-town settings, quirky characters, and a dollop of romance, then you'll enjoy this amateur sleuth mystery series.

Pick up the whole series at https://smarturl.it/maplesyrupmysteries.

ABOUT THE AUTHOR

Emily James grew up watching TV shows like *Matlock*, *Monk*, and *Murder She Wrote*. (It's pure coincidence that they all begin with an M.) It was no surprise to anyone when she turned into a mystery writer.

Alongside being a writer, she's also a wife, an animal lover, and a new artist. She likes coffee and painting and drinking coffee while painting. She also enjoys cooking. She tries not to do that while painting because, well, you shouldn't eat paint.

Emily and her husband share their home with a blue Great Dane, a Boxer-mix, seven cats (all rescues), and a budgie (who is both the littlest and the loudest).

If you'd like to know as soon as Emily's next mystery releases, please join her newsletter list at www. subscribepage.com/cupcakes.

She loves hearing from readers.